MW01535830

the Life of Riley

the Life of Riley

Alexander C. Irvine

SUBTERRANEAN PRESS ✦ 2005

First Edition

ISBN
1-59606-013-1

Subterranean Press
PO Box 190106
Burton, MI 48519

www.subterraneanpress.com

For apocalyptic kooks everywhere

Zena

I met Gabriel Riley in 2031 and lost him three years later. He approached me at a party, and I decided he was all right because he didn't immediately start talking about himself. Which is not to say he didn't spend plenty of time talking about himself later, but that was later. That first night what I remember is a sweetness about him. I had a hard time believing he was with PPS until he showed me his ID, and once I'd seen it I had to wonder what a gentle soul like Bib was doing in that line of work. He never did strike me as the authoritative type.

We were married after only six months, and it wasn't because Bib was the first man I'd met since divorcing Louie Barnard who would stand up to Louie, although that was a nice side effect. We got married out of a desperate need not to be apart. I knew Bib was working for Presidential Protective Services, which meant that he could be shot or incinerated or gassed at the whim of any wacko who wanted to rid the world of President Waldrop, but Louie had been regular Marine, which wasn't anything like PPS. Not even privatized. So marrying into PPS was a step up—which my mother never stopped reminding me—and Bib was a step up from Louie.

The Riley parents didn't come to the wedding, and I was glad. He wasn't speaking to them often, and I didn't want any tension at our little JP wedding at the Alexandria courthouse, with the sun glinting through the smog off the wings of jetliners coming in to National Airport.

Bib had also dropped hints that his mom wasn't exactly bedrock-stable. "I was born at the stroke of midnight on January first of the year two thousand and one. My mother thinks I'm the Second Coming of Christ," he said to me on the one occasion I pinned him down about it. He was serious, but I didn't know if he meant it literally or not. If I'd known...but I didn't, and there's no way I could have. He didn't talk about it. By the time Marie de Montaigne (whose husband Bib had supposedly shot, which is where all of it started, or at least where I started to find out about it) had opened my eyes to a few things, it was all too late. Preordained if you like.

Louie Barnard never could stand the idea that I'd left him, and it didn't take him long to decide that I'd been carrying on with Bib before walking out on him. Once he had that idea fixed in his head, he had it in for Bib, and so when one of the women in my cubicle at GovTek called me over to see Captain Louis Barnard, USMC, on FedTV's *Dan Rather*™ *in the Morning* talking about Bib and a riot, I knew there was going to be real trouble. Then when Lucky Katmanivong called me at work and said he was coming over, I started to be afraid.

Lucky had been Bib's shift partner on the South Lawn beat for about a year then, and the two of them were friends. Both of them were from the Quad

Cities—Lucky a native of Rock Island and Bib a proud son of Moline—and they were the same age. Bib thought they might have played Little League baseball against each other, but he was never sure. I trusted Lucky, and when he said that I should stay put at GovTek until he got there, I did exactly that. When he called again, I was right there at my terminal waiting for him, and when he said that Bib was waiting for me at some lawyer's office out in Stanton Park of all places, I thought to myself *Good, he's gotten himself a lawyer*. That, and the thought that Lucky was involved, made me feel a little better about things, as good as you can feel when your husband is accused of a shooting.

I asked Lucky if he was going to be there.

"Just go meet him, Zena," were his last words before he repeated the address and hung up. I walked right out of the office and caught a cab.

✦✦✦

KAPLAN, NG, ASCHENBRENNER AND NG, read the sign hanging over the glass door. Across the street, three streeties were passed out under the marquee of an abandoned movie theater. Nothing else moved on the block; all of the stores appeared to be closed, and no pedestrians were in sight. The thermometer on my watch said it was 101 degrees, on April 22.

I walked into the office and found a secretary sitting at one of four desks in a book-lined front room. "Can I help you?" the secretary said.

"Yes, I—I'm looking for Gabriel Riley," I stammered. "I was told he'd be here?"

The door opened and shut behind me, and I turned to see the three streeties from the movie theater crowding in. The one in front drew a gun from his coat and pointed it at me. "Mrs. Riley? Can I call you Zena? Why don't you come with us?"

✦✦✦

I am sorry to say that even after everything that happened over the next few days, I still could not bring myself to acknowledge that Dan Rather™ was an android. When Louie Barnard had been on FedTV listing Bib's offenses, and Dan Rather™ himself had nodded gravely before continuing with an on-site reporter, it seemed impossible that Bib could be innocent of the charges against him.

Dan Rather™, I thought. A hundred years old, more, and still the only mouth any member of the Mendez family cared to hear the news from. He looked not a day over seventy, and the rejuv clinics he patronized were instantly top-ranked. Nobody in my family believed the rumors that Dan Rather™ was an android controlled by the Bettys — the aliens were already advisors to the President and Congress, what did they need Dan Rather™ for, the argument went — and my mother had once nearly assaulted Bib for suggesting that the name was now trademarked because it wasn't really a human being behind those piercing eyes any more. "All kinds of people trademark their names!" my mother shouted, brandishing a barbecue fork. "I could trademark my name! Am I an android too?" She had a point: lots of musicians and actors trademarked their names. According to my parents, if Dan Rather™ said something, it was true, and Dan Rather™ said that Bib had shot a Haitian squatter and incited a riot on the South Lawn.

They even flashed a picture of the squatter on the vid: skinny, dreadlocked, dressed like a circus knife-thrower, his arm around a striking woman, much taller than him with her hair pulled severely back. Under it, the caption: *Roi Bertrand de Montaigne.* Dan Rather™, in voice-over, said, "The woman accompanying him in this photograph is his wife Marie." Representatives of the South Lawn squatters were claiming that the shooting was an act of unprovoked brutality, and for once the Marines were agreeing.

I was watching all of this in the break room at GovTek, watching my life scatter and disperse like so many phosphors. Then I went to meet Bib, thinking there must have been some mistake, there must be some way to fix it all; and instead found Lieutenant Fiske.

✦✦✦

It was four days before I really got angry enough to try to get out, which might sound crazy, but you see what you do when Dan Rather™ accuses your husband of inciting a riot on the South Lawn of the White House and then you get kidnapped at gunpoint after your husband's best friend tricks you. Initiative is a fragile thing.

The room they'd put me in was tiny, barely large enough to lie down in, and empty except for a dry double laundry sink on one wall and an open drain in the center of the concrete floor. Insulated pipes ran across the ceiling and down the back wall, near a closet door. On the wall opposite the sink, to the right of the door I'd come in through, a narrow window let in a shaft of pinkish light. Streetlight-colored light, and it was hitting the ceiling, so I figured I was at least on the third story of whatever building I was in.

The man named Fiske hadn't been back in several hours, and I was through being grateful to be alive. They'd fed me, okay, and I hadn't been raped or tied up or tortured, but I was still locked up in this little room God knew where, and I had no idea where Bib was. Much less where I was.

But they didn't know where Bib was either, or if they did they sure were working hard to convince me otherwise. Every couple of hours for the last four days, either Fiske or one of his boys had come in to interrogate me about places where Bib might have gone. What were his normal patterns of behavior?

They did not include shooting Haitian squatters, I told them. So if he has done that, I can't assume that the rest of his actions will be typical, now can I? So I don't see how I can help you.

Fiske was very patient. He had a patient face, and even though he was holding me hostage, I liked the way he spoke and I liked how he didn't move his hands too much.

Where do you think he would go, Fiske asked, if he was in real trouble?

Home, I said. And when he found out I wasn't there, I thought, he'd probably go looking for me. Right then I decided I had to get out of wherever this was Fiske was keeping me. Bib was exactly the type to start barging in, and that was exactly what they wanted.

"This is not exactly standard procedure, is it?" I asked Fiske the last time he came in to grill me. "I mean, it's not exactly kosher to keep a man's wife hostage when you want to question him about a shooting, is it?"

"Zena," he told me, "if you knew how serious this all was, you'd be congratulating us on our restraint."

When he left, I started trying to figure a way out.

I looked the room over, searching both for clues about where I was and anything I might be able to use to get out. Streetlight meant that it was dark out, something that hadn't occurred to me before because the light in my cell was always on and I hadn't found a switch. Maybe the Fisk-ettes had sacked out for the night. I searched in my pockets and came up with my NID card, the scrap of paper bearing the lawyer's address in Stanton Park, a hair elastic and some loose change.

Oho, I thought. Maybe that freshman year in the UVA dorms did me some good after all.

I tied my hair back with the elastic and inspected the door. It was metal, with a heavy deadbolt lock, hardly the typical janitor's-closet fixture. Someone must have put this one on with an eye towards locking people up.

Metal door, that was good. Nobody would be able to kick it down. If the old dormitory trick worked in the real world, I thought I might just be able to get out.

As quietly as I could, I sidled up to the door and listened. No sound came from the other side. Quickly I selected a nickel from my handful of change and tested its width against the crack between door and frame. It jammed tightly about two-thirds of the way in. I only had one more nickel, and after a moment's indecision, I forced it in as far as I could where I thought the deadbolt went into the frame.

None of my other coins were wide enough to stay in the crack, so I dumped them back into my pocket.

I looked at the window again. It stood near the ceiling, held shut by a swivel latch set into the top of its sash. If I could get to it, I thought I might be able to squeeze through.

To what, was the question. The window might open fifty feet above a street, and then what would I do? Jump?

Eyeing the window, I stepped up onto the sink. There would only be one chance at this. If I missed, the noise was bound to bring somebody running. But then I guessed I'd find out how well that old nickel-in-the-door trick worked in the real world; it had sure as hell pissed off Mindy Culpepper when we were eighteen.

"Banzai," I whispered, and stepped forward off the sink onto the doorknob.

Something in the door's frame chirped as all of my hundred and thirty pounds landed on the knob, but I let my momentum carry me forward until I could reach up and grab hold of one of the ceiling pipes. My other foot braced against the wall. So far, so good.

The window latch was rusted, and pulling on it unbalanced my delicate toehold on the doorknob. Still, I had to get the window open; I leaned against the wall on my left and gave the latch a desperate jerk.

It didn't open. Instead the entire mechanism snapped off and clattered to the floor. At the same time my foot slipped off the doorknob, and I barely caught hold of the pipes again. My arms were already trembling from the strain, and I thought I'd heard a noise from the hall.

Bracing both feet on the wall in front of me, I walked up until I could lever a foot onto the windowsill. Then, letting my other foot dangle, I worked my fingernails into the frame and gradually pried the window open.

There were definitely footsteps and voices in the hall now. A key turned in the lock, and my stomach fluttered.

The window opened about sixty degrees, enough to let me through. But hanging like I was, I'd have to go through feet first. Oh God, I thought, now I have to be Spider-Woman.

A bang on the door spurred me forward. I swung my legs one at a time into the opening, shifting my grip on the pipes as my body pivoted and I went ass-first out the window. The door hadn't opened yet, but one of my nickels was hanging on by the barest chord of its circle.

"Zena!" someone shouted. I thought it was Fiske. "Zena, don't do something stupid, now!"

Bit late for advice, now, isn't it, I thought. I slid back and down, the window frame bending under my weight and scraping raw hell out of my belly, until my feet found a ledge. Hooking my arms under the top of the sash, I ducked through the window.

And found myself squatting on a foot-wide ledge five stories above a flooded dead-end street.

"Okay, *chica*," I said softly. "Does whatever a spider can."

I'd been wrong about the streetlight. The light I'd seen came from a shed built on top of a wall to my right. Seeing the wall — the dike — I realized where I was. New York? What the hell was I doing in New York?

Getting the hell out, I answered myself. I stood carefully, keeping one hand hooked in the rusty sash. Through the window I saw the door burst open and Fiske rush in. He spotted me and held up a hand.

"Zena, be reasonable," he said. "You don't want to die."

I spat at him, the first time I'd ever done that in my life. "Why do you think I'm out here?" I growled. Then I kicked at the window, shattering one pane and showering Fiske with broken glass.

"Ow, *dang!* Go, go!" I heard him shout, but I was scooting to my left, away from the window and toward the dike holding back the Hudson River.

✦✦✦

Shadows pooled where the New York authorities hadn't yet replaced burnt-out streetlights, and I ran from one of those to the next in a crazy zigzag, getting to the shed as fast as I could. The doorknob spun loosely in my hand, and I ducked inside wondering how I was going to lock the door against Fiske. Inside the shed, it was pitch-dark except for a fuzzy pink seepage around the door frame, and I couldn't find a deadbolt. All right then, I thought. A second to catch my breath, and then I'd be off again.

To where? I leaned against the cool metal door, listening to the clamor of pumps and what sounded like traffic from somewhere below. I didn't know anyone in New York, and after what Lucky Katmanivong had done to me, I wasn't sure which of my friends I could trust any more. All I could hope was that Bib hadn't found out where I was and come looking for me. It would be the romantic Bib-like thing to do, but I had a feeling even then that if he did it we'd never see each other again.

First things first. I had to make sure I was really free of Fiske and his black-shirted compadres. And Louie Barnard. He was involved in this somehow. Once I got back to Washington and found Bib and took care of whatever mess he'd gotten himself into, that would be the time to worry about revenge.

I looked around the interior of the shed, my eyes adjusting to the near-total darkness. A faint yellow light glowed in a steep stairwell in front of me; the pumping noise and—if I was really hearing it—the hum of passing traffic came from down there. I couldn't go outside just yet, and I didn't feel like waiting to see if Fiske came busting into the shed, so I gripped the handrail tightly and went down the metal-grate steps.

The stairs ended in a catwalk running about eight feet above the floor of a long narrow room lined with pumps and concrete tanks of river water. Maintenance lights hung at thirty-foot intervals, nearly half of them burnt out and the rest haloed in the humid, sewer-stinking air. The catwalk and the soles of my feet thrummed with the constant hammering of the pumps. I'd been right about the traffic noise, too; a deeper rumble through the catwalk could only have been a tractor-trailer passing underneath the floor. They have a road under this wall and all that water? I thought, incredulous. Nobody in their right mind would come anywhere near it. I imagined my *asustona* mother leaping out of the car at the tunnel entrance, trailing bright scarves and curses.

Maybe the catwalk ran all the way to the next shed, however far that was, and I could sneak out there and try to make my way into the city. Even if it didn't, it would get me farther away from Fiske, and I could hide down among the pumps if I had to.

"Yeah, and then what?" My voice was lost amid the noises of the pumphouse. I had seen enough media reports from New York to know what happened to single women who didn't know their way around. Even my mother, who had grown up in the Bronx before following her husband into government work in DC, wouldn't come back. "When I was a girl," Mama said, "the *barrio* was tough, but there were still rules." Her accent always grew thicker when she reminisced, and she would shake her head, face drooping and sad. "No more."

I'd never been to New York before, and I figured
Mama knew what she was talking about. But what
else was I going to do? I hurried down the catwalk,
looking over my shoulder at every noise that jumped
out of the general hammering. As I went, I tried to
piece together a plan that would get me to Bib.

FedTV said Bib shot somebody and started a riot,
but Louie Barnard was involved, so something was
going on that wasn't getting out (at the recurrence of
this thought I felt a deep pang of betrayal; maybe
Dan Rather™ *wasn't* what he used to be). Two: Bib's
partner had made a phone call that led me into a
kidnapping. Three: The kidnappers looked and
sounded military.

It wasn't much, all in all, and it raised more
questions than it answered. Why, if somebody was
trying to set Bib up, had they kidnapped me? The
only thing that made sense was some kind of ransom
exchange, and the Rileys weren't exactly rich. But
then why was the military involved?

What did Bib have that they wanted?

There was a third possibility, of course. Maybe—
I shrank away from the thought—maybe Bib had
really done what he was accused of. Had he gone
crazy, or had one of the squatters attacked him?
Neither scenario explained why Fiske and his men
had come after me, or why Fiske had given his
spooky answer when I'd asked him about it.

I needed to get Fiske in a situation where he had
to tell me what I needed to know, but how?

All I had to bargain with was myself. For some
reason I was valuable to them. I had the ghost of an
idea then, an idea so desperate I thought I must be
crazy for coming up with it. But as I turned it over in
my mind, I couldn't see any other way to get what I
needed out of Fiske. I hurried along, footsteps rattling

the catwalk, hoping I was still the swimmer I'd been when I was nineteen.

✦✦✦

The catwalk did run to another stairwell, and I climbed up into a pumphouse identical, as nearly as I could tell in the dark, to the one I'd first fled into. I felt my way to the door and found it locked.

Feelers of panic began to tickle at my composure. Had I been allowed to escape because they knew I'd duck in here and be cornered? I pictured Fiske and his men lounging back at the first pumphouse, joking and waiting for me to come back out.

That didn't make any sense, though. Why would they let me escape just to capture me again? I had seen enough movies to know that when the bad guys let you escape, it was so they could follow you and see what you did. And in this situation, that wouldn't do Fiske any good, since I had no idea what I was going to do or what they wanted me to do. No, it was simpler to believe in a broken lock and good old military incompetence. Mundane facts of life.

Still, my fingers were unsteady as I searched for a lock and found it, a simple tab in the doorknob that turned counterclockwise. Pressing myself into the wall, I eased the door open an inch. Cracked concrete and rusting railings whose flakes of green paint looked like black blood in the streetlights; I saw no men in black, and the only noise was typical urban background clutter tempered by a sharp breeze off the river. Here goes, I thought, and stepped outside.

"*Bird!*" someone shouted, practically in my ear, and I was caught by the upper arms and pinned against the pumphouse door. High-school self-defense classes went to work like reflexes; I stomped hard on a booted foot, raking my heel down my attacker's shin. Answering shouts echoed from somewhere up the dike, and the panic I'd felt before returned, clamping down on my chest. Twisting against the man's grip, I kicked at him, grazing him once and connecting solidly the second time. Nearly losing my balance as one of his hands let go, I pivoted and drove the stiff fingers of my free hand into his left eye.

"Ahhh, *bitch!*" he howled, his free hand going to his face. Still he held on, hauling me to one side, until I regained my balance and kicked him squarely in the groin. Then I was off and running south again, but not for long; ahead I saw two men running toward me. Pounding footsteps told me others were behind.

Time to see if my idea is crafty or suicidal, I thought. I veered to my right and clambered over the waist-high rail on the river side of the dike. "Stay back, Fiske!" I shouted. "Anyone tries to grab me, I jump!"

They all skidded to a halt maybe twenty feet away, forming a semicircle around the light pole I was using to balance myself. I looked from one to the next, trying to pick out Fiske's face, and with a shock I saw that two of the five men in front of me weren't men at all. Close, but a little too tall, a little to thin, heads a little too big and skin a little too gray under the harsh pink of the streetlights on the dike.

Bettys? I thought. What in God's name is going on here? A cold feeling spread through my stomach as I thought about Dan Rather™ and what people said about him.

Fiske stepped forward, hands held palm-out in front of him and his pale, chubby face flushed from running. "Zena," he said, "calm down now. You don't know what you're doing."

"You stay *back*, Fiske!" I warned. "I know damn well what I'm doing."

"Okay, Zena, what are you going to do? What good does it do any of us if you jump?" Fiske smiled. "Come on now, let's be reasonable."

"Far as I'm concerned, she better fuckin' jump." The man who'd first caught me limped into the circle, one hand still pressed to his eye and the other occasionally making abortive movements toward his groin. "Fact, I think I'll make sure of it."

"Please watch your language," one of the Bettys said.

"Stay back, you son of a bitch." I didn't want to jump yet. I hadn't learned anything. But I couldn't be caught again. No way would they let me escape a second time.

"Private Wright, rejoin the ranks," Fiske ordered. Wright ignored him and the admonishing Betty.

"With all due respect, sir," leered Private Wright, "I am obeying a higher power."

Fine, I thought. I'll swim to goddamn New Jersey if I have to, just so I can come back and kill each of these bastards with my bare hands.

"You wanna lose your other eye, Wright? Is that it?" I taunted. "Or haven't your balls swelled up big enough? Bring it on, big boy. We can swim together, fine with me."

Wright's one-eyed gaze crawled over me like a centipede. He tried to straighten up and couldn't, but he kept shambling toward me. Blood was black on his lips under the streetlights.

"Last warning, Wright! Return to the line!" Fiske's voice, normally televangelist-smooth, rang high with tension.

Wright's gaze didn't waver from me. "Fuck you, Fiske," he said, and then the right side of his head blew apart. I jerked at the sound of the gunshot, hunching down behind the railing with one arm wrapped around the base of the light pole. Wright's body completed a step, then toppled slowly forward, pivoting to land on his right shoulder. With a soft slurping sound that I will never forget as long as I live, part of his brain slid out of his shattered skull to rest on the pavement. He rolled over onto his stomach, let out a long breath, and died.

Fiske reholstered his gun. "Now that's too bad," he said. "See, Zena? No one wants anything bad to happen to you. Now come off the edge there so we can talk."

I couldn't take my eyes off Wright. One of his eyelids was still fluttering. "I don't believe I will," I said. My voice shook, and I shut up.

"The gunfire is likely to draw attention," one of the Bettys said to Fiske.

"Not down here. They'll just think it's the floaters settling their differences."

"Nonetheless, we should resolve this quickly."

"That's up to Mrs. Riley."

I was right, I thought. They need me for something.

"I want to know what's going on here, Fiske," I said in a steadier voice. "Where's my husband? Why'd you kidnap me? And what in God's name are they doing here?" I pointed at the two Bettys.

"Do not blaspheme," they said in unison.

Religious Bettys?

Fiske shot them a look. "Big questions, Zena," he said. "The truth of it is, we don't know where your husband is. We were hoping you could help us out with that. As far as what's going on…well, have you ever wondered why the Bettys are here? I know I have. And thanks to these gentlemen," he indicated the Bettys, "we're beginning to understand. You see, ever since their arrival, people have been falling all over themselves trying to be more like Bettys. They're fashionable, right? But…are you a religious woman, Zena?"

"I go to church," I answered. Fiske nodded as if that was the answer he'd expected.

"Yes. Well, there are those who think the Bettys are angels, did you know that? They think that God sent the Bettys as an example of what humans could become. But what they don't seem to realize, Zena, is that God has already sent his example. Jesus Christ is our example, and we don't need another. Now some of the Bettys themselves came to realize this as well—they accepted the Gospel and found the Lord.

"And you know what happened, Zena? The other Bettys had them arrested. Had them deported in the name of their Law. Well, what higher law is there than to seek the Lord and spread the Gospel? And why are Bettys being arrested once they do that?" Fiske's face had lost all trace of its earlier good humor. Deadly earnest now, he took a step forward and continued. "Does all this seem familiar, Zena? Persecution? Arrest for loving the Lord? Reminds me of the Roman Empire, and Nazi Germany, and Soviet Russia and Red China. That's why the Bettys are here; they show us all the wonder of their *civilization*," Fiske gave the word a sarcastic twist, "so we won't notice that they're taking over. How long will it be before human Christians are being arrested too?"

"Amen," said the Bettys.

I stared dumbfounded at Fiske and the two aliens. I'd thought all this was over money, or a grudge or something. Now Fiske was telling me that some kind of—what? holy war?—was coming. And somehow Bib had something to do with it.

"What—where does Bib come into this?" I asked, keeping my tone neutral.

Fiske shook his head sadly. "Well. I'm sorry to say this, Zena, but your husband has become a dupe. You see, the Bettys don't plan to just swoop down in spaceships and take over. They don't need to. Instead they have a way to—bear with me now—a way to *make humans more like them*. That's been their plan all along. That's the big thing they're not telling. They've tailored a nanovirus to change people, make 'em more like Bettys. A virus that'll make people forget God."

"You're crazy," I blurted, and regretted it.

"Am I?" Fiske was smiling again. "Study your history, Zena. Every time an advanced culture shows up in a more primitive place, what happens? With two hundred men, Cortes destroyed the Aztec empire—two hundred men and a little help from smallpox. See a parallel? Less advanced cultures are doomed to be absorbed, unless they see it coming and take action. Are we supposed to believe that the Bettys won't do what every culture in history has in their position? Look at Indians on reservations, the ones that are still around. That's what we'll be, Zena. If we're even still humans.

"But we're lucky in one respect. Their plan's hit a snag—their virus didn't fire like it was supposed to. They're working on it, you can bet on that, but *God* is working for *us*. He sent us these Bettys who have found the truth, and He has given us time to act. If we do not, we deserve what we get."

"Why don't you just tell people about this?" I asked. Fiske had moved a step closer again, and I eyed him warily. "Why all the spooking around?"

"Would they listen?" Fiske took yet another step, halted when he saw me lean back and drop into a squat. "Look around, Zena. People dressing like Bettys, law schools teaching courses in their Law, college people telling our kids how benevolent and sophisticated Bettys are. People trying to eat Betty food, little girls getting Betty dolls. We—by which I mean not myself and you and these men here, but the big media-aggregate info-linked statistically-sampled American We—want to be like them, you see? Nobody wants to hear that maybe they should be more like us. So our group works behind the scenes, and there are lots of us, Zena, in some very high places. When we act we will be decisive. But we can't act until we find Bib Riley."

"Why?"

"He has something we need. He has the trigger that will start the virus replicating. If he shows it to the wrong person, we're lost already."

"So—" Baffled, I trailed off. What if it was true? Why did Bib have this trigger? Had he been involved in something this big without her knowing? Since when did he have that kind of security clearance?

"What do you mean, he's a dupe?" I said finally.

"He took this trigger without knowing what it was. He was deceived into doing it, promised a lot of money. Bib is blameless, Zena; none of us want to hurt your husband. But we have to make sure that the trigger never gets used. Every soul in the world depends on that."

Fiske came forward again, stopped again when he saw me tense. "Come on, now," he said, reaching out a hand. "Come help us find Bib."

I wavered. Fiske could be telling the truth, and my hamstrings were quivering from the strain of squatting over the twenty-foot drop into the river. Fiske had killed a man to keep me from jumping; would he hurt me if I came back?

No, I thought. But why did he have to kidnap me to tell me this? I would have listened in my living room. And what would happen after he found Bib? Were Fiske and Wright the kind of Christian soldiers I wanted fighting the human race's battles? I looked down at Wright's body, remembering the look on his face before Fiske shot him. Crazy people, I thought. The other side might be crazy too, but that doesn't make this bunch sane.

And even if Fiske was telling me the truth, he wasn't telling me all of it.

I straightened up, my hamstrings twanging, still holding onto the rail with one hand and keeping the other on the light pole. "Thank you for leveling with me, Fiske," I said.

A look of relief passed across Fiske's face. "You deserved to know," he said, reaching to help me back onto the dike.

"I'm going to go find my husband now," I said, and let go of the railing.

✦✦✦

The soles of my sneakers broke the river's surface with a sharp crack, swallowed instantly by the gurgle of bubbles and the muffled mechanical heartbeat of pumps as the force of my fall drove me deep into the chill water. Sudden turbulence caught me and tumbled me backwards, and I thrashed against if before the words of a lifeguard ex-boyfriend came back to me: *If you ever lose track of which way is up, stop. Your legs'll sink first.* I did, and my body righted itself as the swirling rush faded to a gentle Jacuzzi-like kneading. From my left I heard the muted thrum of traffic in the West Side Tunnel as I kicked toward the surface.

The lights on the dike seemed more irregular than they had up close, and farther away; how far could that undercurrent have dragged me? I shook water from my eyes, taking deep slow breaths and treading water as quietly as I could. To my left, other lights drew my attention, along with urgent voices. I'd been turned around; that was the dike over there, with the PetroMerica Empire State Building standing sentry beyond it.

A flashlight beam swung my way and I slipped beneath the surface, watching until the beam passed overhead. Eyes stinging from God knew what poisons in the water, I bobbed back up. I was maybe fifty yards out from the wall, close enough to be seen, and even if Fiske didn't spot me right away, he'd have boats out soon enough. Downriver, to the south, what were those lights? I wasn't sure at this distance whether they marked the edge of the island itself or something out in the river. Pleasure boaters, perhaps. It was a nice night, I guessed, if you weren't floating in the Hudson River escaping an interspecies gang of armed religious freaks.

I kicked off my shoes and struggled out of my jeans, thanking God that fashions had come around to loose again; Fiske had been right about the Bettys' influence there. I struck out for the distant lights in a rhythmic breaststroke. When I thought I was beyond earshot, I went to a steady crawl, letting the current boost me toward the flickering lights.

✦✦✦

I wasn't in the shape I'd been in at nineteen, that was for sure. It took two rest stops of sculling on my back and ragged panting before I was close enough to see that the lights I was making for were fires burning on the decks of a cabled-together agglomeration of barges and houseboats. The whole scene reminded me of the South Lawn squatters' camp. Breaststroking again, I swam closer and came up against a steel mesh barricade rising at least twenty feet out of the water.

Easy enough just to climb it, I thought, even with my arms turned to rubber. The nearest boat, a listing old tug, was less than a hundred feet way. People thronged the decks of the cordoned-off armada, passing bottles around the various bonfires and pursuing children when they careened too near railings and gunwales. All of them were black, and the voices that reached me were an exuberant babble of French, Spanish, and lilting Caribbean English. Might as well live it up, I thought, when the only way you get off the boat is deportation or prison. I hooked my toes in the mesh and rested, not sure yet if I wanted to be seen.

Clearly I couldn't stay hanging like a tree frog on this barricade. If the boat people had been fenced in, there would be patrols to make sure that they didn't get out. The average cop would just pitch me inside — story or no story, pigment or no pigment — and then I'd really be stuck. Fiske would find Bib and then...I didn't know what would happen then, but I didn't intend to let it happen the way Fiske planned. Maybe I could go under the fence, if it didn't go all the way down?

Filling my protesting lungs one more time, I let myself sink, keeping one hand on the mesh and tapping below me with outstretched toes. When I ran out of air, I still hadn't found either a gap in the fence or the river bottom, and I came back up, not sure if I should — or could — try again.

As I broke the surface, a light pinned me and I heard the slap of water against the side of a boat.

Trying to draw a quick breath, I sucked in water, but I dove again anyway, choking out the last of my air as the light probed the water around me. Forced to surface, I coughed up a lungful of river and started climbing the mesh barricade.

Someone splashed into the river behind me and strong arms locked around my waist. I struggled, but I couldn't let go of the fence to strike at the man dragging on me or his weight would pull me into the water. The flashlight went out, leaving only a dim glow from the bonfires to see by.

"Zena, don't," a woman's voice called, urgency clipping the Caribbean roll of her vowels. "If you go over the top, patrols will come. There are sensors."

Still I thrashed against the man pulling me back, breath whistling in my waterlogged lungs. The steel mesh cut into my finger and toes, but I managed to climb a step.

"You won't find Sergeant Bib if we are all arrested," the woman said.

I stopped trying to climb, but I kept my aching fingers hooked in the fence. The man holding me let go and slipped back into the water. I looked over my shoulder and saw a black woman in a rubber raft, her hands on the oars as she leaned forward and said, "Zena, please. We've been looking for you all night." In the water at the base of the barricade floated a bearded Rastafarian, smiling in the firelight, his salt-and-pepper dreadlocks spread out about him like the tentacles of a Holstein octopus.

Something about her face tickled my mind, and after a minute I got hold of it. "You're his wife," I said. "That squatter Bib shot. I mean didn't shoot."

"Somebody shot him all right," the woman said. "Your friend Lucky."

I tried to work that out and couldn't. Water dripped into my eyes, and all I could think to say was, "You know where Bib is?" My exhausted mind grappled with the situation—Creole-sounding Rasta deportees knowing who I was, finding me here, knowing about Bib—and gave up. Whatever was going on, I was just too tired to fight any more.

The man in the water lifted one arm. "Come down, Zena Riley," he said. "We don't have time."

✦✦✦

I rested against the barricade while the two Jamaicans deflated the raft. "The hole in the fence is over here," the woman said, and they led me away from the looming dike. "This is Ato. Take my hand; the hole is a ways down."

We sank downward and squeezed through a loose flap in the mesh. On the other side three men waited in a rowboat. Ato and Marie boosted me into the boat and swam alongside until they docked against a huge old ferry moored to the dike.

By the time I'd climbed the rope ladder dropped from the ferry's deck, I was shivering in my soaked T-shirt and underwear. "We must get you dressed and dry," Marie said. She led me into what must once have been a dining area, closing a sliding door behind us. "Back in a minute," she said, and went through a curtain into an adjoining room.

Still shivering, I collapsed into a lounge chair at a low circular glass table. An unused bar took up the wall to my left, extending to the doorway Marie had gone through. Other glass tables, most cracked or with crooked wedges split away, refracted the rug's red and purple pattern in unsettling ways. The room didn't seem like a living space. Other than a decrepit, abandoned shipboard bar, it didn't really seem like anything at all. Why had Marie brought me here?

Marie returned with a towel, an old sweatshirt and long skirt, and a steaming bowl of spicy fish chowder. I dried off and changed quickly, grateful for the clothes even though a prickle ran up my spine at putting on a stranger's things. Just the way I was raised. I managed to ignore the feeling long enough to tuck into the soup.

"This is a meeting room now," Marie said, wrapping a woolen shawl around my shoulders. The dry clothes and chowder began to warm me, and my shivering subsided. "We rarely meet formally so it isn't used much. I thought you would prefer to avoid crowds."

"Thank you," I said with my mouth full. "For everything." A few bites later, I slowed down enough to ask, "How do you know about Bib?"

"He shot my husband," Marie said, and I froze with the spoon halfway to her mouth. Damn, damn, damn, I thought.

"You said it was Lucky," I said.

But Marie just smiled. "It's not what you think," she said. "I'm not angry. Bertrand, my husband, put him up to it."

"Put him up to it?" I set down my spoon. "You mean, *asked* Bib to shoot him?" Getting answers was a hell of a thing sometimes.

Marie nodded.

"Is he okay? Your husband, I mean."

"He will be."

"Well..." I was stuck for something to say. "Why?"

"Mm," Marie said. "That is the question, isn't it?"

A teapot whistled, and Marie got up and disappeared behind the curtain again. She returned with the teapot and two mugs on a wooden serving tray, apologizing for the lack of sugar like we were just two friends having a Monday lunch together. Now that I wasn't afraid of drowning any more, I found myself bursting with questions. Where was Bib? Was he okay? What was he mixed up in? How could she find him before Fiske did? I bit them all back and waited for Marie to tell me what was going on. I would get it all sooner or later, and at least Fiske hadn't found Bib yet.

The tea poured, Marie sat back in her chair and said, "What did Fiske tell you?"

"He said Bib was a dupe. That he — Bib — had been fooled into doing something he shouldn't have done."

"That much may be true." Marie's eyes were downcast, her voice quiet and mournful. "And if it is, I am to blame."

I could hear the story now, lying unspoken behind Marie's disconsolate words. "Maybe you should tell me why," I said.

✦✦✦

It is terrible when someone comes to you and tells you that a loved one has died. But it is even worse, terribly worse, to have that person himself walk up to you and say *Now I must go and die.* When I saw Bib again, the day after Marie and Ato found me hanging from their perimeter fence, this is what happened.

We had only a moment together before he learned the truth about what he had to do, and I hated every tick of that time even though I could not bear to think of it ending. When he came up out of the stairwell with Nate Drinkwater and the mountain of a man I only ever knew as Mike, I was out of my chair and sobbing into his stubbly jaw before he had both feet on the deck. He ran his fingers over my hair and down my back, and he twitched away from me when I touched a bandage behind his left ear.

The first thing I could think of to say was, "Of all the stupid ideas. A million dollars for a squatter's pass."

"Well, if Louie Barnard hadn't been such a prick," Bib said. He kissed both my eyebrows, and he had tears in his eyes too, and his voice constricted to a whisper as he hugged me close again. "I was so afraid you were dead."

I flinched at the words and took a step back, running my hands along his arms. "There's — we have to tell you some things," I said, and all the life bled out of my voice. I found it hard to breathe.

Bib looked back and forth between me and Marie. "What?" he said. "Bad news?"

Mike interrupted. "Time for me to get moving," he said. He extended a hairy hand to Bib, his face set in an expression I wished I couldn't read. "Sergeant Riley," he said, "I want you to know that I only lied to you as much as I had to."

Bib shook his hand. "Okay," he said.

"Did what I could." Mike's tone of voice said he wasn't sure it had been enough. He opened the door. "Have to go see a man about a truck," he said, and left.

Marie locked the door behind him. "People don't knock around here. Sergeant Bib, you know Nathan, and this," she indicated, "is the Counselor."

The Counselor was a smallish Betty, broader-featured than most and jittery. He put down a piece of paper he'd been shredding and stood. "Gabriel Riley," he said formally. "I wish our acquaintance had come under more auspicious circumstances."

"Seems pretty auspicious to me," Bib said, reaching to take my hand. "I don't have the permit, but I've got my wife." I squeezed tightly and put my other hand over my mouth. Bib watched my face, and uncertainty appeared in his. "Unless there's something everybody's not telling me," he said, looking from Nate to Marie to the Counselor to me.

✦✦✦

An hour later, he stood with me looking from the top of the ship out over the crazy-quilt jumble of the Squatter Regatta and the dilapidated, smog-blurred warrens of Jersey City. The Hudson River was a rich earthy color under a scorching morning sun. Around us, vegetables and wildflowers grew in carefully-arranged plots of river sediments dredged up a bucket at a time. Bees hummed among the flowers, and seagulls perched eagerly on the railing now that Marie had shooed the gardeners away, following them down the steps with a half-hearted admonition that Bib and I should keep the gulls away from the tomatoes.

"Funny thing is," Bib said, watching a butterfly alight on a raspberry bush, "I was pissed off about that shot all morning. Hurt like hell."

I stared disconsolately out over the river. "Nothing about this is funny."

"Mama would be so proud," Bib said, letting his mouth run because he couldn't say anything that would make me feel better. It was something he always did, and it might have been endearing at any moment other than that one. "Eighteen years of my life she told me I was some kind of Messiah, and now I guess I've got my chance, don't I?"

"Got your chance for what?" I snapped, angry tears springing into my eyes. "Who knows what the Bettys have cooked up? He could have told us anything, he could have lied. This—" My mouth wouldn't form the word *virus*. "This *thing* you've got, if you go meet this Truman person, how do you know things will happen like he says they will? These people fooled *Dan Rather™*, Bib, they fooled everyone; *how do you know?"*

I cast about for more words, then slumped against the railing. "Isn't there someplace we could go?" I asked brokenly.

Bib reached out to me, resting a hand against my cheek. "Honey," he said, "I don't know if they're telling the truth. I think they probably are; it would explain a lot. But there's no place we can go now. If this Truman's been in New York all morning, there's probably a million carriers now. And they'll spread it, and if I just get within sneezing distance of one of them..." He left it there.

"We won't be human any more," I whispered, leaning back into Bib. "Don't we deserve a chance to work out our own problems?"

"Yeah. Yeah, we do." He kissed the top of my head. "And we're gonna get it."

I turned around. "What?"

I listened to the buzz of the bees, the rustle of gulls settling watchfully on the rail, and I did not want him to say what I knew he would say next.

"I'll go meet Truman," Bib said.

I stood a long time, looking out over the river but not seeing anything. "Oh, Jesus," I said finally. "Isn't there a better way?"

"There isn't any other way at all. We have to be sure, and if either one of us is still around it'll never be sure. Marie said that there's riots going on, people wanting the Bettys gone. Maybe they won't come back, and...hell, maybe we'll learn something." It all sounded so weak, like a cheap moral. A cheap excuse.

Any way you looked at it, the Bettys seemed right, and *that* was wrong.

How many chances *have* we had to learn something? I thought. It's a miracle we have any choice at all. If Bib had gotten to New York on his own, wandered around, it would be too late already. Marie and Mike knew what they were doing, I guess.

"If I ever see your mother again," I said, "I think I will kill her."

There was no good way for Bib to react to that, so he didn't.

I leaned into him again. "It wasn't—" I began, then started over. "You know, I only married you so I could laugh when you were a foulmouthed old curmudgeon falling into his pants in a rocking chair."

"Yeah, well, when I looked at you I always saw a dotty old grandma with a yard full of hummingbird feeders and a—a Batman flyswatter." Bib's voice broke and he cried into my hair.

Wordlessly I held him, rocking him back and forth, stroking the back of his neck. "I don't want to do this," Bib wept. "I don't want to *have to decide* to do this."

"But you do." I lifted his chin, wiped at the tears on his cheeks. I made an effort to smile. "I love you too, but I can't have any foulmouthed old curmudgeon who won't do the right thing when he knows he has to."

We turned together at the sound of footsteps on the stairs. Nate and Marie came up, Marie hanging back as Nate limped up to Bib and nodded at me.

"Fucking Counselor thinks he's got it all figured out," Nate said. "You're not gonna do it, are you?"

"Not the way he thinks I am." Bib wiped at his eyes. "Even if I was, I think Mike's got something on the back burner." A strange calm settled over Bib.

Whistling past the graveyard, I thought. Only he's buried there, too.

"Yeah." Nate shook his head. "Army-surplus weirdos." He shifted his weight uncomfortably. "I'll go with you, Bib. You haven't been down in the Oracle, and this is the wrong time to get lost."

"No," Bib said. "Bad enough I have to do this. I'm not taking someone else with me."

"You misunderstand me. What I meant was I'll lead you to the place and get the hell out." Nate scratched at his beard. "All I seem to do lately, lead you from place to place."

"And get me in goddamn trouble." They shared a short laugh until I interrupted.

"For God's sake, *go*," I said, embracing Bib, feeling the hard beat of his heart against mine. He started to speak, but whatever it was, he cut it off.

I pulled back and kissed him. "Go," I said again. I stayed there in the garden as Marie led them back down the stairs.

✦✦✦

Marie and I walked on either side of the Counselor, guiding him to the stern of the grounded cruise ship. A turbo helicopter waited there, its rotors spinning idly half in and half out of the shadow of the dike.

A rolling boom came from the north, and I turned to see a column of smoke and dust rise above the dike. A frothing dome rose in the river near the spot where I'd jumped in the night before, and I heard the sustained rumble of a collapsing building. Cars began to heave up to the surface of the river; a city bus, its windshield shattered and its roof partially caved in, rode briefly across the dome before turning over and sinking out of sight. The dome rose still further, then subsided as the dike, incredibly, began to buckle. A fifty-meter section of it collapsed, and the Hudson River rushed into the gap.

Bib was dead.

"You will regret this," the Counselor rasped. "Lives were sacrificed to complete the work you have just destroyed."

I turned on him. "People sacrificed their lives to destroy your work, *Cousin*," I said. "Why do you think we care so much? Did you ever think that you should have asked us what we *wanted?* Are we Cousins, or is it more like idiot siblings?"

A tremble started in my voice, and my hands were shaking too. "My husband *died* because you felt *guilty*, Counselor. And how many other people over there," I waved the gun I'd forgotten I was carrying in the direction of the rising column of smoke over 33rd Street, "are dying right now because you couldn't treat us like human beings?"

He said nothing, and after a moment I realized he wasn't going to. I dropped my arm and turned away from him.

"Get off my planet, *alien*," I said.

Someone shouted from the direction of the helicopter. I whirled, hearing gunshots, and saw the Counselor take a step backwards. The Betty's arms waved behind him as he lost his balance, and he fell slowly to the deck. His legs moved slowly in a scissors motion, as if receiving a belated command to run.

Lucky Katmanivong stepped under the helicopter's tail rotor, service sidearm held in front of him. He walked slowly, purposefully, to the Counselor and shot the dying alien three times in the head.

"Your fault," he said, and I saw that he was crying.

Looking up, Lucky saw me; his gaze twitched to his left and he raised his gun again.

But the gunshot I'd heard came from behind me. I ducked, falling to my hands and knees on the splintery wood deck. Lucky doubled over as if mimicking me, sinking down to a squat. Blood stained his green pants black and began to drip onto his boots.

Marie walked into my field of vision. "It was not his fault, Lucky," she said gently. "If you must blame someone, blame me."

Lucky moaned and sat down. Looking directly at me, he said, "I'd do the same thing again."

"Walk away, Lucky," I answered, "or I will kill you. Go away and die somewhere else."

"It doesn't matter where I die," Lucky said.

I cocked my gun.

Never taking his eyes off my face, Lucky struggled to his feet. Instinct to survive, I thought. Is that what this Project was about?

"I figured something out, Zena." Lucky tossed his gun over the rail into the river and held up his bloody hands. "No matter what, Project or no, someone takes it in the—in the gut." He gasped a laugh. "Five hundred years ago, your parents; sixty years ago, mine. Next time someone else. But it always happens.

"You go ahead and shoot me if you want," he finished, turning his back on me and walking painfully toward the helicopter.

I watched him go. It cannot be that we only survive at each other's expense, I thought. I refuse to believe that.

I refuse to believe Bib died for that.

The Counselor

I t was very strange, this being on a different world. Strangest of all that things were similar enough to the Home World for comparisons to be drawn, although this should have been expected. The strangeness itself was strange, because if one thought about it, things that were truly foreign to one's experience — as a different planet, with sentient life, should have been — did not seem strange. They were too remote for any common ground, and thus too remote for parallels.

An infinite regress, the Administrator said to me when I confided this in her. Or an indiscernible boundary, which amounts to the same thing.

May my phase change soon.

Different sounds, odors, colors: everything was odd, bent somehow, but by what I couldn't say. The laws of the sensual world had never held my interest; anything that could be discovered (interesting word, that, in English; "made naked") through so imprecise a means as experimentation was of only tangential consequence to the mind. The laws of the mind were the real work.

Even so, I took pleasure in the view from the Administrator's lofty office overlooking the Mall. Sunset burst a brilliant red in the blanket of mechanical effluvium draped over the Potomac Valley. A dark red, only seen in thickened air such as this, beautiful the way a toxin-induced hallucination was beautiful. Under the smog, also beautiful in an uncomfortable way, the human city sprawled to the limits of vision.

So, too, did the Administrator's Cousin-related problems. The agent of her current discomfort was one of the People (Bettys, the humans called us, for some unfathomable reason), but this Person seemed to have become enamored of — infected by, one might almost say — human ideas. Part of the Administrator's task this evening was to determine the extent of the infection, and my entire task was to assist her in her work.

I considered phase change, releasing a solid lump of anger in my mind to slowly dissipate into the white noise of my background thoughts. The Administrator too was angry, though she did not speak of it. To see the Cousins, the Saviors, so debased...surely the algorithm had been faulty. Surely an aberration had been introduced. An aberration that might reveal itself through the conversation that was about to take place.

The Person standing before the Administrator's desk had adopted human dress, a reversal of the norm. The dress of the People had become hugely fashionable among the Cousins, refining the likeness between them to an extent that made the Administrator and myself profoundly uncomfortable.

"Will you require the use of a name?" the Administrator asked. Despite the circumstances, she was determined that protocol would be observed.

Civilization exists only as long as rules are followed, and in that light protocols of address carry the same weight as any other law.

Proscription of treasonous acts, for instance. Including acts of colonization.

The Person held his breath briefly, then let it out in a slow hiss. "What is said to one is said to all," he said.

"Your cooperation is noted." The Administrator relaxed slightly at the Person's compliance. I too grew less tense, although it was still difficult for me to remain still. Facilities for a trial did not exist this far from the Home World, and the Law provided that an Accused Person could demand a trial before a full tribunal. Either this Accused planned to challenge the Law on other grounds, or he had no desire to mount such a challenge.

Gesturing for the Accused to sit in the chair facing her desk, the Administrator activated a desktop recorder and began the interrogation. "Is it your contention," she asked, "that your presence here was coerced in an unlawful manner?"

"It is my contention that the Law you refer to is corrupt, and therefore coercive. Laws of the world betray themselves when they attempt to govern the spirit."

"The People contend that the actions which precipitated this proceeding have far more to do with temporal power than spiritual progress."

"'Thy kingdom come, Thy will be done, on Earth as it is in Heaven.'" The Accused Person crossed himself and sat in the chair facing the Administrator's desk.

The Christian gesture, and Christian words, shocked me. *Does this Person genuinely believe? Can that be possible?* A physical assault would have been less disturbing.

Solid, liquid, gas. The serenity of phase; what changes, changes back. I could see the verse passing through the Administrator's mind as it passed through mine. She refocused herself on the Protocol. "Pursuant to the Law regarding interference in native cultural affairs, this proceeding will be conducted in English, that the wronged native parties shall understand the workings of the Law."

"And I am the one who is to be charged with an act of colonialism?" the Accused spat. "I see the Law has provided for its own subversion in the cause of its perpetuation."

"The Law is made available for those who wish to learn it," the Administrator replied with remarkable restraint. "You are charged with conspiring to interfere in the course of a native population's development. This charge is compounded by the further offense of doing so by taking advantage of native religious beliefs."

"And how does the Law distinguish between my alleged offense and the Project which brought the People here? Is not the Project interference in the course of Cousin development?"

"The Project is to restore the Cousins to their proper course, not co-opt their superstitions in the service of political gain."

"Does not the fact that the Cousins were originally set on their course by the People negate the contention that they are a native species?"

"It does not. Had the Error not occurred, your contention would merit consideration, but it is clear that the Error has altered the Cousins to the point of merging them firmly in the terrestrial ecology. Thus, even if they were not originally a native population, they must be considered one now."

"The Error, as you call it, is what has made them human," the Accused said. He stood. "This proceeding is farcical, and I stand ready to refute any charge that my belief in Our Lord and Savior Jesus Christ is political or insincere." The Accused placed the tips of his fingers on his right temple and recited, "'I believe in one God, the Father Almighty, maker of heaven and earth, and of all things visible and invisible; and in one Lord Jesus Christ, the only begotten Son of God...'"

A fanatic, then. I repressed a physical shudder, aware that a camera recorded our every action and that proper conduct of this interrogation was essential to the success of the Mission.

There will be no subversion of the Law as long as I am assigned to the Administrator, I vowed. To subvert the Law is to erode the civilization of the People.

But if the Accused (who continued reciting the Christian affirmation) had genuinely adopted Christianity, the problem was even more severe than we had intuited. The Mission commanded the recovery for the Cousins of their true place in the universe, to make amends for the Expulsion so long ago. You can lead a horse to water, I thought, remembering a human proverb that said more about primate psychology than equine.

The Accused Person finished his recitation and sat silently.

"The People note that the Accused neither denied the charges nor offered mitigating circumstances other than an avowal of religious faith. The charges are therefore considered to be substantiated." The Administrator paused to consider her course of action. Obviously deportation to the Home World was the proper decision; we had discussed this at length before calling the Accused in. The only question was whether to enforce a quarantine on the

Accused until such time as he could be shipped offworld.

"'An unjust law is no law at all,'" the Accused quoted. "Even the humans have known this for centuries. If the corruption of the Law is not a mitigating circumstance, this Person would defy the Administrator to determine what is."

Here was the crux of the matter. To what extent were we bound by the letter of the Law to interfere with its intention?

Events had gained too much momentum. The Administrator in her perspicacity saw this. Only one course of action had any hope of salvaging the Project in its original form.

"That question is possibly valid, but it certainly lies beyond the purview of a single Administrator," she said. "Revisions of the Law can only be undertaken by the Judges on the Home World. If you wish to pursue your claim, you must do so upon your return there.

"And, pursuant to the previously-cited Law regarding interference in native affairs, the People sentence the Accused to immediate return to the Home World. Further, the Accused is prohibited from contact with humans until it shall be determined that the Accused is no longer a threat to the Mission we undertake on this world. Does the Accused understand this sentence?"

"I do, and as is my right, I appeal."

"Such is indeed your right," the Administrator said. We had planned for this occurrence, but even so what she was about to do sickened me. The spirit of the Law was not to be abused in the execution of its letter, but the Administrator could see no other way.

"Your appeal will be heard immediately upon your return to the Home World."

The Accused shot to his feet. When he spoke, his voice had shed the last pretense of civility. "A direct violation of the Law! I demand that another Administrator hear my appeal before the sentence is executed!"

Solid, liquid, gas, I thought. But there are intermediate states, are there not? Surely this is one.

Surely we are doing the right thing.

"The nature of your offense," the Administrator said slowly, knowing that Scholars on the Home World would dissect her every inflection, "precludes any certainty that your appeal would be heard by a disinterested party. The extent of the conspiracy — to which your silence is taken as confession — is not known, and all other Administrators on this world are therefore suspect. Therefore the only possible venue for your appeal is the Home World itself."

"Corruption suppurates in your words, Administrator," the Accused sneered. "As it does in the words of the Law."

"My words are the words of the Law," the Administrator replied, barely keeping her composure. "Your analogy is circular. And your offense is unprecedented; the History of the People records numerous attempts by individuals to interfere with native populations, but none in which a Person has used adoption of native religion as rationale for such interference. In the absence of precedent, I am compelled to act first to protect the integrity of the Mission. Your actions are a threat to the Mission, and your sentence therefore stands, with appeal to be conducted on the Home World."

The Accused composed himself and sat down again. "In much the same way," he said, "were the Apostles persecuted. You stone me with legalisms, and crucify me on the cross of soulless words. But know you that the cause has grown, too much for Law to stop it, and at the final trumpet call, you will be judged under the Law of Laws. 'By thy words thou shalt be condemned.'"

"Let the sentence be carried out," the Administrator said. I opened her office door and admitted two People designated to conduct the Accused to a quarantine room until a vessel could be made ready.

The first guard approached the Accused and said, "The Law dictates that you may be nonfatally harmed should you attempt to escape our custody, and fatally harmed should you attempt to injure either of us. Are you cognizant of the Law?"

The Accused rose and faced the guard. "In condemning me, you condemn yourselves." He looked back at me, then let his gaze linger malignantly on the Administrator. "All of you."

The two guards followed him as he stalked from the room.

We sat quietly for several minutes after they were gone. The sun had set, and the streets of Washington, DC were lined by bright lights as if signaling the path of a nocturnal diaspora. The Washington Monument indicated the sky like an idiot child seeing stars for the first time.

You condemn yourself. The words hung in the air, and I wondered if the Accused had not been right. The Administrator's actions, after all, had exploited the letter of Law — in point of fact the absence thereof — in possible contravention of its spirit.

She spoke as if reading my thoughts. "Officiousness is the first step towards corruption, is it not?"

"No," I said. "We are charged with protecting the Mission, and protect the Mission we will. The Home

World supports us in this; otherwise they would not have sent the Program by such unorthodox means. Desperation on the part of the Home World calls for a certain degree of zealotry here."

The Administrator and I were the only People on Earth who knew of the Program, and that knowledge was heavy. She rarely suffered from indecisions, but she did not share the certitude of her superiors on the Home World that it would correct the Error. No one, it seemed, was prepared to say exactly what the Error had been, or whether it had occurred during the Cousins' Journey or after they had been exposed to the terrestrial environment. Nonetheless the Home World was calmly insistent that the Program would do as they intended.

"I have just charged a Person with violating the Law," the Administrator said, "and yet I am complicit in an analogous violation myself. If the Program fails, will I myself be Accused?"

"No," I answered. "We operate at the behest of the Home World and in adherence to our charge of protecting the Mission. What better motive than Restoration of the Cousins?"

Solid, liquid, gas. These were certainties.

In between, though, living bodies incorporated all three states. And the actions of living beings fell between certainties, into the flux of mind.

The plan to execute the Program had already been set in motion, and to interfere with it would be to sabotage the Mission. The conspiracy of which the Accused had been a part threatened to do exactly that; and because neither I nor the Administrator could be certain which of the People were complicit, the Administrator had broken the Law by guiding the actions of human agents. The People she had chosen for the task of issuing the Command were being killed, and none had been able to directly approach the Vector, Truman Throckmorton. Fortunately all of the murdered People had been able to destroy their Commands before agents of the conspiracy acquired them, but I never knew the Administrator to have confidence in fortune. She had come to believe that only human agents would slip through the fine mesh of the conspirators' net.

Thus the Mission and the Law had come into conflict, and she had only her own judgment to go on. Her own judgment, and secretive machinations more appropriate to war than a mission of mercy.

"Gabriel Riley," she said softly. She had forgotten I was there, and I suffered both at being forgotten and at her uncertainty. "I hope I have not misjudged you. And I hope I have not misjudged the Law."

✦✦✦

Later that evening the Administrator called me into her apartments. During the eighteen hours since the Trigger had been removed from Washington, DC, intelligence had arrived in fragments, like dust that lacked the density to coalesce into a planetary body, tantalizing her with hints of a conspiracy whose upper reaches neither she nor I could see. The more we learned, the less we knew; we were reduced to constructing similes. Again, an infinite regress.

Clearly the Administrator faced concerted opposition to her task of rectifying the Error, and the scope of that opposition seemed to broaden with every dispatch she deciphered. Still, the only concrete information she had was an address, a lawyer's office somewhere east of the Mall. A rendezvous was to take place there in three days' time, but who would be there and what the purpose of the gathering was...the answers to those questions were liquid, changing shape according to how we framed the scenario in our ongoing policy discussions. Blind grasping after understanding found only deeper incomprehension, just as liquid seized in a fist squirted away to soak into the soil of this strange Homelike world. Another simile, another indirect admission that we were playing a game whose rules changed with every move.

Hints of opposition to the Project — coming first from still-anonymous Cousins, oddly enough — had been surfacing for well over a local year. The Administrator had tried to stay her course through the storm of intrigue without enlisting Cousin assistance except as backup measures, to be held in reserve in the event of catastrophic failure. Now it was beginning to appear as if those backup measures were all we had to operate with. If the Administrator could not ascertain which People were corrupted, she had no choice but to operate using exclusively Cousin agents, and each of those had to have a carefully monitored information intake.

In those few moments when she could force her mind to release the intractable problems of her position, she confided in me her curiosity regarding how much the Cousins understood of their origin. In some nations — indeed, some areas of what was still called the United States — their educators were still criminalized for daring to contravene religious orthodoxy. Even 200 years after their first glimpse of evolutionary biology, a significant fraction of the Cousins believed themselves to have been created whole by a supernatural deity, never mind the infinitely regressive ontology such an idea demanded. It all seemed sometimes like a species-wide case of psychological distress of the sort observed in abandoned children.

The grasping after certainty when the universe so clearly denied it, the wholesale sacrifice of the planetary ecosystem in the name of status and luxury, the irrational resistance to population control — all seemed to indicate a fanatical desire not just to survive, but to blow trumpet fanfare into the ears of a deaf universe. The Cousins' shortsighted tunnel vision had already driven them to the threshold of ecological collapse.

We had talked of this too many times for anything of value to emerge from the conversation. The Administrator shook her head. Of course it was easy to play Wise Elder when we knew the truth about the Cousins' origin. They were very young, and the long view could only be learned when perspective had enlarged enough to grasp it. We would have to guard against letting our superior knowledge mutate into an assumed racial superiority. Paternalism would achieve nothing; the Project would be completed for its own sake, or not at all.

"But is that not evangelism of a sort, the same evangelism that I Accused and Banished another Person over just this afternoon?" she asked me.

I had no answer.

Intermediate states. Shades of gray, as the humans would say. More accurately, as the Americans would say; in addition to guarding against racial chauvinism, the Administrator continually had to remind herself not to take Americans synecdochically to represent all humans. People were present in most of Earth's reasonably stable nation-states, but as Senior Administrator, the task of executing the Project had fallen to her. Reports from her colleagues indicated that there were several states on Earth within whose borders the speaking of English was a capital crime, and motion-picture theaters in Paris and Hong Kong had recently been burned for showing revivals of fifty-year-old American films. All of which made execution of the Project even more crucial; the fangs-bared nationalism that took aesthetics as its battleground recalled the episodes of the People's history that had brought both races to this juncture.

Our knowledge, and our willingness to act, were all that could restore the Cousins. The Administrator and I both believed this, although our outlooks on the Project's success differed sharply. Is it chauvinism to acknowledge reality? To accept responsibility for the actions of ancestors?

Some things, after all, must be absolutes.

"This meeting," she said when I had entered her apartments and run a security screening. "What is to be done?" It was unusual and disconcerting for her to ask me so openly for advice; I saw with perfect clarity that the Administrator's callous manipulation of the Law in her interrogation of the Accused Person had been motivated—and, she hoped, mitigated—by genuine concern. In the face of a conspiracy that violated Law and the Project, she had no way of knowing who among the People had been corrupted. Certain of her advisors, she felt—including me—were trustworthy, but mistaken assumptions would be devastating. And enlisting further help from the Cousins was an equally uncertain enterprise.

"Send someone," I said.

"Perhaps myself."

"Absolutely not. If some of the People have been infected with Cousin religious extremism, what sort of Cousins must they be dealing with? You must not be risked when the outcome of a meeting is so uncertain."

"Your concern dignifies you, Counselor," the Administrator said. "Yet I believe that we possess enough information to minimize the danger of my attendance."

"We have a location and a password. I fail to understand how this qualifies as sufficient when we do not know who else will be there."

"Whoever else will be there, they will know something about Gabriel Riley," the Administrator said. "It is imperative that we find out where he is."

I withheld my initial objections and concentrated on observing protocols. "If this is to be a policy discussion, a recording should be made."

"Make no recording. I cannot trust the security apparatus."

In the silence that followed, I became conscious of how lonely the Administrator must feel.

She broke the silence. "The request I am about to make is nonstandard and should take place outside normal protocols."

"Understood," I answered. I placed my deactivated personal recorder on the Administrator's desk.

She nodded at the gesture. "Elements of the People's Mission have entered into a clandestine effort to subvert the Project. In doing so, they have contravened numerous sections of the Law. You are no doubt aware of the Cousins' tendency to construct religions incorporating mysterious visitors from the skies?"

I nodded. "They are hardly unique in that," he said.

"Agreed. Thus we have Law prohibiting any Person from taking advantage of such beliefs for personal gain. Unfortunately this is precisely what is happening."

"The offenders must be prosecuted," I said simply. Even in an unrecorded meeting taking place well into the night, Law and protocol were foremost in my mind. Those, and the imperative to serve the Administrator.

"Indeed they should," she said. "But the situation is complicated by the apparent fact that certain of the People have in fact adopted the Cousin religion known broadly as Christianity. The messianic tenor of this religion leads converted People to readily sacrifice themselves if such sacrifice will preserve the identity of their co-conspirators."

Completely unwarranted extrapolation, I thought, based on a sample of one. But worst-case scenarios were in this case appropriate.

"Then the scope of the conspiracy is not known," I said. I cast a glance at my recorder, wishing that I could transcribe these revelations and pass them along to the Home World.

"The Home World has been made aware of the conspiracy," the Administrator said, "and measures have been taken. The efficacy of those measures, however, is uncertain, and it is therefore important that information-gathering efforts proceed."

"You speak of this meeting again." She nodded. "Would it not be more prudent simply to arrest and interrogate everyone present? The situation justifies some compromise of liberty."

"Agreed. But most, if not all, of those present will likely be Cousins." The People had no legal authority over indigenous populations. "The possibility exists," the Administrator continued, "that my arrest order would find its way to the conspirators themselves, and then not only would no arrests be made, but the extent of my knowledge would be revealed. I find it more prudent to indulge a small risk to my personal safety in order to gain more precise information about the goals of the conspiracy."

The logic of this was difficult to refute, but I struggled. The personal safety of the Administrator had, in my mind, long since ceased to be a completely rational concern. I looked over her shoulder, out the window into the humid night.

Abednego, I thought. That was the password we had intercepted in our search for Gabriel Riley. A name from religious myth, one more laboratory-created element unsuited to the real world.

"Reluctantly agreed," I finally said. "What will you require of me?"

"Simply to monitor my actions. I will notify you when I leave to attend the meeting, and again when I return. Should six hours elapse with no word of my return, assume that my return is improbable and take what measures you deem justified."

The implications of her last statement hung in the air. I could have dissuaded her. Perhaps things would not have turned out as they did.

My choice was made long before, when I entered the Service and opted to define myself by my value to my superiors. "Understood." I moved toward the door, then paused. "Administrator: I feel bound to offer an alternative. Would it not perhaps be more reasonable simply to abort the Project and wait for time to erase this conspiracy? In a few generations the Cousins forget even their own ancestors. During that time, action could be taken...?"

She smiled at me, perhaps envious at my easy cowardice. I was out of my depth here. Solid, liquid, gas, I thought; and where is the People's philosophy and protocol when intermediate states stubbornly impose themselves? When Law failed, individuals stumbled along as best they could.

"Too much has already been set in motion," the Administrator said, just as I had gathered myself to repeat the question. "Even if the People left tomorrow, the Project would continue. It is incumbent upon us to see it to its conclusion. Also it is my responsibility to discover which of the People have turned against the Project."

"Understood," I said again.

The decision made, we suspended discussions to eat. Homesickness always afflicted the Administrator at the end of a workday. Even on the Home World, where I had watched her since her early academy studies, she had never been socially inclined outside of family, and here loneliness and the daunting scope of the Project combined to sap her energy. Synthesized meals, wistful communications from her partner and child, a room looking out over the Potomac estuary, night after night that found her in exactly this spot with three hours before dawn and no one but me for company. I shared her fatigue and her loneliness, and during those shared moments I found empathy with those of the People who had abandoned the Project, even for those who had moved into human communities, subsisting on nutritional supplements and the few terrestrial foods that the People could metabolize. Even (I had heard) entering into sexual relationships with the Cousins, nonprocreative of course, but disturbing all the same.

The Administrator's empathy, though, went far deeper than my own. It had led her to turn a blind eye towards such infractions, believing that they constituted a needed outlet for those of the People who otherwise would have presented more serious problems for the Project. Perhaps she had been correct in that assessment, but it now appeared that her laxity had allowed germination of the conspiracy that now threatened the Project.

The Administrator broke into my reverie. "I marvel at the Cousins' history," she said. "So rife with individuals leaving everything behind, going to foreign places in the name of religion or science or politics. Perhaps their first great journey prepared them for such endeavors. Three million years is a long time."

"Time enough for changes beyond the Error," I said. She did not answer.

A ping from the constituter drew her attention. She retrieved our meal and we ate. My mind was in turmoil, and whatever pleasure I took from the food was unconscious, analogous to the pleasure photosynthesis might provide a green plant.

A chirp from the Administrator's personal communications terminal drew her attention from her plate. She went to the console to bring up the new message, and I watched her. She looked puzzled for a moment, then sat heavily in the console chair, rocking it backward.

I stood to see what had so affected her. On the screen, the message text was simple:

THE FURNACE DOOR DOESN'T ALWAYS OPEN AGAIN.

"Who has done this?" the Administrator wondered aloud.

On the screen, the anonymous message glowed in the room's near-darkness. Immediately the Administrator ran a trace, but the hound she sent returned with no information. Was her office, her *person*, under surveillance? I feared for her, and incidentally for myself. She stared at the words for a long time, then deleted the message and shut off the terminal.

THE FURNACE DOOR DOESN'T ALWAYS OPEN AGAIN.

Ironic that myth can be so much more potent than simple truth.

We were no longer the pursuers. Now we were being led. The danger to the Administrator was greater than we had realized, but so was the imperative to uncover the conspirators.

"I will go to the meeting," she said softly.

"They are expecting you." Odd, how shock impoverishes my language.

"The Project is larger than any one Person," she said. "I have no choice but to attend this meeting, and hope that I can make some use of what will be revealed there." She turned the console chair to the window and sat silently. Together we watched the stars lose themselves in the approaching predawn storm.

✦✦✦

I caught occasional glimpses of my own face, fearful and ill at ease, in the automobile's rearview mirror as I chauffeured the Administrator through downtown Washington's twenty-four-hour crush of automobiles, bicycles and blinkered pedestrians. The next lane to our left was nearly empty, reserved for official and diplomatic traffic, but the Administrator had insisted that we travel in an anonymous civilian car. Having me drive her was her single concession to the possible danger of the situation. When she and the other Administrators had refused bodyguards two years ago, the Cousin protective services — whose minds seemed incapable of thought beyond scenarios of assassination and violent revolution — had insisted so theatrically that all Administrative Counselors go through courses in evasive driving and physical combat that the Administrator had given in to placate them. Although thin and no longer young, I knew enough about unarmed confrontation to disarm most wild-eyed terrorists.

I fervently hoped none of those skills would be called on this night. Or ever. The Administrator sat in the back seat wearing the standard disguise of the People — human business suit, head scarf and wraparound sunglasses, meant to look like a sunlight sensitive Cousin — looking out through the polarized windows. I thought I could see misgivings akin to my own on her face.

I wondered if my partner and children would find me inscrutable when I returned to the Home World. A period of readjustment was inevitable, of course; prestige was not without cost, and the position of Administrative Counselor was nothing if not prestigious. My problems, whatever they turned out to be, would be trivial compared to the difficulties encountered by Persons born off-World when they came to the Home World for the first time. After even a handful of generations off-World, such easily malleable phenotypic features as height and pigmentation were vastly changed, much to the consternation of the insular bureaucrats who populated the Home World. Differences in dialect also appeared, although contact between the Home World and the far-flung outposts of the People's civilization remained frequent enough that even a Person whose family had left the Home World a hundred generations ago could conduct a conversation. The differences, though, became so large so quickly...

And the Cousins had been gone for more than three million of their years.

"Concern for your well-being compels a question, Administrator," I said.

"Speak, Counselor," she said. "Your concern is appreciated."

"You are certain of this course of action? I have thought on this, and it still seems to me that safer alternatives might be considered that would yield similar results."

"Possible," she said. The same could be said of the entire Project, though; it could easily be what the Cousins called a fool's errand. Indeed, were it not for the unprecedented nature of selected Persons' treachery in this instance, I believe that the Administrator herself might have suggested a less forceful intervention. The presence of enemies had a way of clarifying a situation, though, and the recent emergency measures taken by the Cousin agents in Iowa limited her options.

"Law is not to be hidden behind," she said. "Anomalous situations must be dealt with as such. Intermediate states must be experienced, embraced." She did not go on, but I had heard the rest of the proposition before, in my own schooling. *Because the only perfect equilibrium is death.*

And the Cousins were certainly approaching that point. With scarcely the technology to reach their planet's satellite, they had driven the terrestrial ecology to the point of collapse. In a very few years, their ten billion would be reduced to less than half that, if the typical process of overpopulation and catastrophic die-back was not forestalled by technological innovation. But machines could only delay the inevitable; the collapse would come all the same, unless the Project proved successful.

You see, Cousins, I thought, we have come to save you. Because you haven't the will to save yourselves. We owe you at least that much.

I spoke again. "Consider what I have said. You are essential to the Project. The danger you put yourself in may be counterproductive."

"The Project will continue regardless of my participation," the Administrator replied. "It has accumulated enough momentum to survive. If something be saved through its subversion."

I said nothing more until we pulled to a halt behind a battered gasoline-burning van sputtering blue smoke in front of the building where the meeting was to take place. In this part of the city, at this time of night, vehicle traffic was sparse and pedestrians nonexistent.

"Remember what I have said, Counselor." The Administrator opened her door. "You may yet have to act on your own."

"Understood." I turned to look at her through the window, and my voice rasped slightly as I spoke. "Caution. Do not endanger yourself needlessly."

"When the People are turning against the Law, there is no needless danger," she said. Then she shut the door and hurried across the sidewalk.

Sometimes the furnace door doesn't open again, I thought.

The monitor she carried on her person had only audio capabilities. I heard the click of the door latch as she entered the deserted office building, and then a voice: "Lock the door behind you."

After a moment, I recognized the voice. A male named Mike, large and unkempt and in my opinion dangerous despite the Administrator's previous utilization of him as a source of intelligence.

"Am I to consider this a betrayal?" the Administrator asked. Mike's previous actions on her behalf — and Gabriel Riley's — had not led us to believe him involved in the conspiracy. Perhaps our analysis had been lacking.

"Betrayal of what?" Mike said. "I needed to talk to you, and I'm not sure the other channels are any good now. I didn't call this meeting, if that's what you want to know."

"Is there a problem with the First Vector?" The Administrator's voice shook slightly. If there was, if Mike had turned on her, on the Project....

Mike barked a short laugh. "You're missing the point. Far as I know, everything on that end is going according to plan. But some other things ain't the same, and that's—"

Everything on that end is going according to plan. I felt a surge of optimism at this reassurance that the Vector was moving, but Mike's explanation was cut off by the bang of an opening door.

"Sit down, Betty," a Cousin said, using their slang for the People. "That chair there's fine. You, fat boy, pull up your shirt. Right, the redneck holster." The Cousin snorted.

"Fuck you, Louie," Mike said. Louie? Louis Barnard? This was a catastrophe. We knew Barnard to be involved with those of the People who had adopted Cousin religion, and we knew him to be pursuing Gabriel Riley.

"Surprised you can find it under that gut," Barnard said. "Gun on the floor, two fingers and slow. Then sit next to Betty over there."

I heard a groan as Mike settled his weight on a wooden chair. "Didn't bring no backup, Louie," he said. "You grow balls?"

"Haven't needed backup yet," Barnard gloated. "Old Betty here did exactly what I thought she'd do. You got worries, don't you, Betty? Things aren't going how you'd like them to. Well, your troubles are just beginning. Where's Bib Riley?"

"Who you asking?" Mike said.

"Shut the fuck up, fat boy," Barnard said. "You, Betty. Where's Bib Riley?"

"I do not know," the Administrator said. My mind raced through possibilities; when I had heard

Mike's voice, I had assumed he was there to update us on Riley's location. Now it occurred to me that he might have come to ask the Administrator, that he might have been duped just as we apparently had.

"Your boy got away, huh?" Barnard said. "Don't think I believe you. Am I not being persuasive enough?"

I opened the car door. There were firearms in the room, and I had no idea what I might be able to do, but I could not sit while the Administrator's life was being so nakedly threatened.

The side door of the van in front of my car rumbled open and four Cousins emerged. Two carried stubby firearms. I recognized one of them, a female named LaWanda. Gabriel Riley's mother. Her presence baffled me utterly. They went to the front door and opened it with a key. I heard the key turn in the lock, and heard one of the four say, "Abednego," as the door shut behind them.

"Goddamn, it's the OK Corral in here," Mike said.

"Shut up, fat boy," Barnard said. He stood. "Took you long enough," he said to the new arrivals. "I though I said midnight sharp."

"We're all on God's time, Captain Barnard."

"Speak for yourself, Henry. God doesn't wind my watch."

"Mm-hm," Henry said serenely. "You'll come around soon enough." Soft footsteps. "And what are you, creature?" he asked. "We'll soon find out."

"I should warn you," the Administrator said, "that my disappearance will not go unremarked."

"Oh, I'm counting on that," Henry replied. "You reappearance won't either, believe you me. By then we'll just see how well your alien act holds together. Well, Sister Riley? Shall we?"

One of the men who'd come in with him interrupted. "I don't want that thing in the van with me, Henry. It's a demon."

"Sam," Henry chided gently, "we've been over this, haven't we? Hasn't the Lord seen us this far? And don't you think He'll see us back home?"

Sam didn't respond.

"Enough with the sermons, Henry," Barnard said. "We've been here too long already. Take the Betty and move it."

"I ain't touching it," Sam said.

"That's fine, Sam," Henry soothed. "Go on and open up the van, then. What do you call yourself?"

"I am an Administrator."

"Well, we'll call you Abednego the Administrator. Come on, Sister Riley, let's escort Abednego here to the furnace. Brother Eric, kindly keep an eye on things."

There was a bang from the back room and a thunder of voices and banging footsteps. "*A screaming comes across the sky!*" someone shouted, then a series of gunshots erupted. I cringed in the seat, paralyzed by the knowledge that already I might be too late to fulfill my duty to the Administrator and the Project.

For a long moment there was no sound in the room other than the rattle of fallen bits of ceiling tile and the frenzied wheeze of Cousins breathing. Then LaWanda Riley said, "Gabriel?"

"Mama?" came the answer.

A shotgun boomed, and my eardrums nearly ruptured at the concussion of a brief fusillade. The office's windows shattered. Seconds later the four Cousins spilled out of the office with the Administrator and another Cousin. I could see no wound on the Administrator, but one of the armed Cousins was speckled with blood, and their captive's clothing was dark with it. They all climbed into the van, and with a belch of unburned gasoline drove away.

✦✦✦

I followed the van out of the city and into the broken hills of Maryland, seething as I ran through an unchanging number of unintelligent possibilities. I could call the authorities, and cause an exchange of gunfire in which the Administrator and others could be killed; I could follow the van until it had to refuel, and betray my unarmed and solitary presence; I could utilize my reluctantly learned driving skills and run the van off the road, possibly injuring or killing everyone in it.

The Cousin captured by the four fanatics was not Gabriel Riley. I had seen him clearly enough to be certain of that. Who was he, then, and what was their interest in him? Was Riley alive? He and Barnard and Mike had not emerged from the office. Where had they come from? Had they been waiting together? It seemed impossible.

How much had the Administrator withheld from me?

We moved toward the Pennsylvania border, along a rural highway. I stayed far enough behind the van to avoid notice as I tried to make all of the facts fit into a coherent pattern. Barnard had clearly monitored the Administrator's communications with Mike, and must have had help in doing so, possibly from the Cousins now kidnapping the Administrator. The kidnapped Cousin had entered with Riley, and might know where he was going. It seemed likely that Barnard had either captured Riley or fallen victim to the exchange of gunfire in the office.

I should have stayed at the office to find out whether Riley was still there, but my loyalty to the Administrator overwhelmed my broader sense of duty. I make no apology for this, since as events unfolded it became evident that my remaining there would have served no purpose. My decision was badly taken but correct.

How it pains me to say that, knowing what I have not yet told.

The decision to act came without volition on my part. I am no uncritical believer in the value of intuition, but I believe to this moment that by acting on intuition I saved the Project.

I accelerated until I was level with the van, and waited for them to see me.

The next moments are unclear in my memory. Several times a firearm discharged from within the van, but although both passenger-side windows of my car disintegrated I received no wounds. I drove the van onto the shoulder of the road; it swerved back; I collided deliberately with it near the front wheel well, and then it slewed away from me, teetered on two wheels, and began to roll. Before it had come to a halt, fire bloomed from its open rear doors.

✦✦✦

I brought the automobile to a shuddering halt and forced my hands to let go of the wheel. Leaning back in the seat, I waited for the stress hormones to tremble their way out through my fingers and toes before taking a last deep breath and getting out into the rain. Broken window glass fell from my clothing to rattle on the pavement.

I was stopped near the crest of a gentle rise in the road, a sort of saddle between two steeper hills. A

hundred meters or so back down the slope, dull fire
flickered in the wreck of the van I had just run off the
road.

And how did I do that? Had I become so
immersed in the Cousins' culture that I could act like
a hero from their video fictions? Is this what
happened when we remove ourselves from our
People and go among the debased amnesiac Cousins?

I had nearly died there; the automobile was
riddled with holes from the kidnappers' guns. I could
not imagine how anyone might have survived the
van's crash, and I began to mourn the Administrator.

As I drew closer to the burning van, a figure
staggered away from it. A female Cousin, I saw, face
blistered and eyes bright with shock. A survivor. She
stopped in front of me and blinked. LaWanda, I
remembered. Gabriel Riley's mother.

"Thought Sam shot you," she said. "And how'd
you get untied?"

The Cousin had mistaken me for the Administrator, a misapprehension only a Cousin could
suffer. As sensitive as they were to differences among
themselves, they seemed to think that all of the
People had been stamped from a mold somewhere.
But the first thing the Cousin had said—had the
Administrator been shot?

If she had, then the Cousins who died in the crash
had died needlessly, for I had provoked it only in a
desperate effort to save her.

Absurd, to be feeling guilt over a group of mur-
derous lawbreakers whose own actions precipitated
their fate, but I was pained nonetheless. It was not
my function to influence things so directly. I am a
conduit, a facilitator, and comfortable as such. I am
not some vigilante hero.

But apparently I had been, and a failed one at that. I walked away from the Cousin toward to the crash site.

"The furnace door doesn't always open again," the Cousin called after me. "I knew that would draw you. You'n me got more in common than you might think. This ain't over, Mister Alien. You wait and see what else I do."

I made no answer. At my feet lay the sprawled body of another Cousin, eyes rolled to the side as if he were sighting down the yellow strip at the side of the road. The look of living things when they have died…a quiet tremor of revulsion choked me, but I lacked the energy to shudder. Belatedly it occurred to me that I should find out what the female Cousin was talking about—furnace doors?—and I turned to ask her. She was gone.

Authorities would arrive soon. We were not on a main road, but still it would be well to hurry. First, though, I must make sure no one has survived. *Administrator, do you live?* It did not seem probable. Still, in an infinite universe…

A quick glance inside the van told me that no one was alive there. Low fire still burned in the upholstered seats, scorching the body of another Cousin, this one lying with charred legs dangling out the van's open sliding door. I turned away and picked my way through the rain along the path the van had taken, wishing for a portable light or even a bright moon. But the rain fell in a steady downpour, sizzling on the van's blackened frame and damping any other sound I might have heard except for water rushing in a drainage ditch just below me to my left.

I found the Administrator next, and for a long dangerous moment my mind fractured into several fragments, shouting each other down, none able to understand the others. I wished to leave, to have never come, to have never enlisted in the Service. I wanted the Cousins to solve their own problems. I wanted the Cousins to obliterate themselves. I wanted to consummate the Project immediately, to rid myself of the obligation the People had assumed. I wanted not to believe that the Administrator had been murdered by the Cousins she'd come to assist, to restore to their heritage.

But wanting was flux, and the Person lying trussed in the weeds at my feet had found her final equilibrium.

You were right, Administrator, I thought. The Project must continue, and Law is not always sufficient to govern the indeterminacy of life. Could I not have learned this another way, though? I looked back on my doubts, my diffidence, and realized how inadequate my understanding of the situation had been. I was growing old, and from the comfort of a bureaucrat's chair had allowed myself to view the Administrator's zeal as youthful excess, bound to be tempered by experience. She had been so vibrant, so certain…and though I looked on her with aging eyes, my longing was very young.

Silly, of course. She had a family, and I too, and nothing would ever have resulted. But some things may not be done for family or belief or cause. Some things may only be done for love. Standing over her remains, I groaned with unexpected grief and swore that as penance for my doubts I would devote myself to seeing the Project to fruition.

Splashing drew my attention to the flooded ditch. Someone alive? Four abductors, two victims…I had seen one survivor and three corpses.

I clambered down the bank of the ditch toward the sound, my progress illuminated only by the dying fire in the van. By that meager light I saw a Cousin half-submerged in the swollen stream. The Cousin's arms were tied; he tried to wriggle up the bank and slipped, sliding into the water. The current pulled him under.

I lost my footing as I tried to move sideways along the bank, and I too slid into the rushing water. Catching at a bush, I arrested my progress before I had gone completely in, but the current dragged at my clothing, preventing me from getting my legs under me. With my free arm, I flailed in the shallows, looking for anything to hold onto.

Instead my hand closed on heavy cloth. The Cousin, but how could I pull anyone free when I was barely able to stand myself? I held on nonetheless, water splashing into my face as the Cousin's spasmodic drowning jerks pulled me down with him.

There; my right foot braced against something solid, a root. With all my strength I hauled on the weakening Cousin, just managing to pull his head free of the water.

"Nnnggahhhh*fuck!*" the Cousin gagged, sucking in air and rain and choking up silty runoff. Kicking me sharply in the ankle, the Cousin braced his own feet on the root and heaved himself with a grunt up onto the bank. He lay there whooping and wheezing, and I worked my own way out of the water, holding onto the bush until I had scrambled nearly back to the level roadside. Below me, the Cousin choked up more water and profanity.

Both of us rested for a moment as the rain grew heavier, coming down in stinging fat drops. Then the Cousin called, "Cut me loose, man. I want out of here."

"I have nothing sharp," I answered, out of breath. "This situation...was unanticipated."

The Cousin craned his neck to look at me. "Kee-rist," he said, "there *was* a Betty in the car. I thought old Brother Sam had just lost it."

Not knowing how to respond, I said, "There may be a knife in my automobile."

"I got one in my pocket," the Cousin responded. "Left front, if the water didn't get it."

Lying on my stomach lest I slide down the bank again, I rummaged in the Cousin's pockets until I located a folding pocketknife. I cut the Cousin free and helped him up the bank.

"Thanks, Mister Betty," the Cousin wheezed. He hacked, bringing up more water.

The slang term discomfited me. "Call me Counselor," I said.

"I'm Nate. Let's get the hell out of here."

"My automobile is this way." I set off up the rise. After a few steps I noticed that the Cousin was lagging behind. "Are you injured?" I asked. In retrospect, this seems a ridiculous question, but I knew no protocol for flaming automobile accidents and midnight rescues.

"Holes in my goddamn legs," Nate growled. "Motherfuckers."

I went back to him, and the taller Cousin draped a sopping arm around my shoulders. Together we made our way to the bullet-riddled diplomatic vehicle. It started immediately, and I turned back toward Washington, DC. I checked the time; less than ten minutes had elapsed since the crash.

"Use the telecom to call in the accident," I said. "I do not wish to have my voice recorded."

Nate did so, giving a vague location based on road signs and signing off before the dispatcher could ask questions. "Nobody's alive back there anyway," he muttered after he broke the connection.

"Not true. I saw the woman," I said.

"You did? Old LaWanda? I wonder what she'll do now." Nate pushed his seat all the way back, straightening his legs with a pained grunt.

"I will see to your medical attention," I said. "It would be best if these events were not made public." I was punching a second access code into the telecom, to arrange for the removal of the Administrator's body. How quickly we begin to cope. Even before we begin to want to.

"Fine with me. What I'd say, nobody would believe anyway."

"Why is that?" I swung onto the interstate and accelerated toward the outer ring of Washington's suburbs, visible as a pink glow beneath the heavy clouds.

"Oh, I talked to your buddy about our little *problem* a couple million years ago. He set this lapsed Catholic boy straight, I'll tell you that."

Behind Nate's bravado, I could see that he was deeply shaken, unsure how to assimilate the information he'd been given. And who would not be? What would the People do if a race from the stars suddenly spun us a similar story?

"She," I said, knowing it was inappropriate but unable to help myself.

"What?"

"The Person you conversed with was female," I said. "She was—very important."

"That's exactly how she described Bib Riley, Mr. Counselor. 'Very important.'" For several seconds, Nate's mouth worked soundlessly. When he spoke, it was in a gathering rush of words as if something long held back had broken loose. "What's with all these very important people, man, spilling the secrets of the fucking universe to old bums like me who don't want to know? Huh? What's with that?" Nate's voice gave out and he began quietly to cry, covering his face with hands still caked with mud and traces of blood.

I did nothing, made no effort to sympathize that might be misconstrued as false or inappropriate. My thoughts, though, were not sympathetic at all. Are you really so myopic? I wondered. Can you really confuse the question of your own origins with the origins of the universe? But the Cousin was too emotionally exhausted to discuss such questions.

"How much were you told?" I asked eventually, when it seemed that a proper interval had elapsed.

Nate wiped his eyes roughly. Twigs and grass were caught in his beard, and his drying hair had begun to curl in the humidity. Pathetic figure that he was, though, I could see that there was strength in this Cousin. He'd been dealt a difficult blow, what with kidnapping, gunshot wound, accident and revelation all in an evening, and here he was rolling down the window and rubbing cold rain into his face. A survivor.

Pulling his head back into the car, Nate finger-combed his hair and angled the car's heating vents up to his face. "You got some fucking explaining to do," he said, leaning back in his seat, and then he fell asleep.

✦✦✦

When he awoke, I explained, and he told me what he knew of events in New York. We went there, and although it reflects badly on my capabilities I admit that Marie de Montaigne found us before we even knew to look for her. She had already found Zena Riley; her perseverance and understanding humble me.

Knowing what I now know, I feel it is appropriate to make reference to the old Cousin religious symbol of wheels within wheels. Louis Barnard was working with the cohort of fanatical People the Administrator had tried to root out, as well as Gabriel's partner Lucky Katmanivong; Marie and Mike were working toward the same ends even as they opposed Barnard and his adjutant Fiske; and of course Gabriel Riley's mother LaWanda had her own agenda despite her and her church's nominal affiliation with Barnard. Conspiracies are ever thus; those who wish to keep secrets in the end must keep them even from colleagues.

If I had known of Truman Throckmorton earlier, I might have dissuaded the Administrator from attending the meeting at the deserted lawyer's office. It seems probable that Riley would have met Throckmorton through the machinations of the various factions. The Administrator need not have endangered herself. That she did is, I submit, testimony to her unimpeachable dedication to the Project, which as I finish this report draws near to fruition.

It is a great day for the People, and the glimmering of a new dawn for the Cousins. I am proud to have participated. Yet I must make explicit confession of my numerous transgressions of the Law.

I have released destabilizing secrets into an aboriginal population.

I have stood by while my superior took unlawful actions.

I have engaged in physical violence resulting in the deaths of three Cousins.

I have placed personal loyalty above dedication to the Project.

In my defense, I argue that had I not done these things, the Project would have failed. We have been so certain of our rectitude. Perhaps the Cousins, in all of their irrational, myopic tribal ferocity, have something to teach us.

I will amend this report when I have met Riley. That meeting is due to take place momentarily. I look forward to it with great anticipation.

Truman

On Wednesdays, Truman Throckmorton always started walking at noon. The Narrow Path Salvation Church was nine miles away, across the Rock Island railroad bridge and through the deserted streets of Davenport, then out beyond the I-280 bypass where West Locust Street turned into state road F65. Not that there was a state of Iowa any more, not really. But the signs helped Truman remember the way. The trip took four hours, depending on the river, and it was like walking through the Cities of the Plain, if they had been destroyed by water rather than fire; empty buildings looking on broken streets, their doorways vomiting fans of black muck that stank and hardened like glue. Truman liked to stop on the bridge for lunch, to fortify himself for the trek through the abandoned city. Bread, cheese, and carefully filtered water was his fare, taken while he dangled his legs under the guardrail and watched the Mississippi, the mighty brown surge the Indians had called Father of Waters. He always looked west, with the much-diminished sliver of Rock Island to his right. Lock and Dam Number Fifteen still held, but the river had carved a new path around it, carrying away the National Cemetery on the eastern end of the island and drowning the Arsenal, whose suspicious buildings still hunched within their breached walls like old bums with old-bum secrets. Truman Throckmorton knew a great many secrets.

The wall clock read eleven fifty-five. Truman peered out of his single window. Fourth Street was dry, although swirling fractal tracks of silt testified to the periodic flooding. Dried mud hung in teary globs from second-story windowsills. Thus far, the river had never reached the third story, where Truman had lived since before the Evacuation. And he knew it never would; he had made his peace with the river and learned the secrets it kept from everyone else.

Truman was almost certainly the last inhabitant of Rock Island, Illinois. The disaster-relief people had tried repeatedly to relocate him after it became clear, in 2021, that five-hundred-year floods now came with the change of seasons. He had refused them then, and again in '24, '26 and 2027, the year of the New New Madrid earthquake and the First Vision. Those who remained in the Quad Cities after the earthquake greeted FEMA with cocked rifles, and the Feds backed down. The refugees streaming from St. Louis and Memphis were more than they could handle anyway.

So Truman had been alone seven years now — although a few people still lived over in Bettendorf and Moline — and that was how he preferred it. The river brought him what he needed to eat, and the fewer people he met, the fewer diseases he could catch. He suspected he was immune to the more virulent microbes, but it would be imprudent to take chances when great things surely awaited him. Not the least of these would be the Second Vision.

The First Vision had been given to him on May 26, 2027. Before that was Bicycle Time. That day, the earthquake had destroyed the cities downriver, heralding the Rapture as surely as trumpets from on high. Truman had awakened from a dream of white noise, tumbled from his cot by the first booming heave. Looking up, he had seen the wall clock stop, then spring from its perch to jitterbug across the bare linoleum floor. The curtains fell like scales from the dusty window and he scrambled clumsily toward the flickering light they revealed.

Outside, Fourth Street writhed like a serpent, illuminated by the spastic glare of lightning. A crushing rain deluged the street and washed over the fractured sidewalk. Power lines spat and crackled, their electricity arcing upward to join the ball lightning that skipped across the rooftops.

A second shock came, pitching him face-first into the windowsill. The impact dulled his vision and a deep distant bell tolled in his head; the edge of the sill broke his front teeth off at the gumline. Sharp fragments of broken tooth tore his gums.

Truman blinked and spat blood. As his vision cleared he saw the river churning, boiling, whirling in all directions as it heaved up from its bed. An eddy grew into a whirlpool at the western edge of Rock Island, and the whirlpool exploded into steam as a great light fell from the sky and buried itself in the riverbed. A vast hole yawned among the steam and mud, and from it came the rushing of the river, and from it came the light that burned into his eyes but would not let him look away, and from it came the voice of God.

I am here, the voice said, hidden behind the brilliant light. *My source is here. From here I flow and it is here I return. I am the unseen life of things and I am their grave. I come from nothing, but you may find me anywhere.*

Watch for me and wait, Truman Throckmorton. Attend on me, for I shall come again.

The whirlpool disappeared and the light faded, leaving Truman to blink at afterimages that seemed to dance at the edge of comprehension. Lightning flared in blinding counterpoint to the subsiding tremors, and Truman collapsed exhausted to the floor. There he saw the clock, half-buried beneath a litter of books and ceiling plaster. "Alpha and Omega," he said. "None shall know the day or the hour." The hands of the clock quivered, then began their slow track across its dusty face. I have to go to the river, Truman thought, but instead he sank into unconsciousness with the bell echoing in his head.

✦✦✦

But today was Wednesday. Truman shook his head and ran his tongue over the space of gum where his upper teeth had been. "Incisors," he said. "It's good to remember the Vision, good to keep it fresh, like a flame, like a lover far away." The Second Vision was coming. He was sure of it.

The wall clock read twelve thirty-three. He would have to hurry, but it was good to remember the Vision, good to keep it fresh, like ice cream, like prophecy. The river would give him its secrets.

✦✦✦

Lunch tasted good on the bridge this Wednesday, with the river surging beneath the crooked pilings of the railroad bridge that crossed Sylvan Slough, Rock Island, and then the Father of Waters. The waters that spoke with the voice of the Father. In Davenport, the tracks led through downtown, then curved north past Fejervary Park and the zoo before crossing West Locust Avenue. From there the walk was long and straight, plenty of time for sunburn and careful contemplation.

"Good to go over the directions in your head," Truman said to the river. "Keeps them fresh, like milk in a petri dish."

Motion across the river caught Truman's attention. A Jeep pulled into the buckled parking lot of the collapsed Rock Island Convention Center. Truman kept absolutely still — when was the last time he'd seen a car moving through the streets of Rock Island?

A man stood in the back of the Jeep and raised binoculars to his eyes. Slowly, purposefully, he scanned the waterfront on the Iowa side of the river, moving from downstream up toward the flooded Arsenal. Sunlight glinted on the binoculars' lenses as the man turned toward Truman.

And stopped.

"You aren't supposed to be watching me," Truman said softly. He sat very still, his left thumbnail carving a gouge in the square of cheese he had for lunch.

The man kept watching, and Truman counted. Five seconds, ten, twenty, thirty full seconds before he lowered the binoculars and sat down in the back of the Jeep again. Its engine roared back to life and it bucked its way out of the Convention Center parking lot. Truman watched to see where it would go; he caught a glimpse of it going north on Fourth Street, then lost sight of it.

"Not supposed to be watching me," Truman said again. "I'm supposed to be watching you, and the only thing I'm supposed to be watching is over there." He pointed in the direction of Sylvan Slough, where the hole in the river bottom had opened.

The Slough split the kidney shape of Rock Island off from the Illinois mainland. From where Truman sat now, the spot was just downstream. About where 25th Street petered out into the western end of the railyards.

After the earthquake had passed, Truman remembered standing in the twisted shadow of the Rock Island bridge, staring at the water rushing over the spot like nothing had happened. He hadn't yet been certain that it was actually God who had spoken.

But then, as if answering Truman's doubts, the voice came again. *Take, drink, Truman,* it said. *This river is my blood; drink it in remembrance of me.*

Truman had, the water stinging his lacerated mouth. And when he had drunk his fill from gentle shoreline eddies, he baptized himself, since no one else was there to do it for him.

"Every man is his own pastor," he'd said to the river then, and he spoke to it again now.

"Woolgathering again," he said, remembering that it was Wednesday, and that the Narrow Path Salvation Church was still a good eight miles away. "Good to keep things fresh, but let's not forget what's under our feet."

Truman got up and folded his lunch bag into his pocket, feeling instinctively for the palm-sized New Testament he always kept in that same pocket. Then he caught himself. "What's under our feet," he repeated, saving the Gospels for the other side of the skeletal bridge.

✦✦✦

This was Wednesday, and Wednesday was a special day, but this day was special even for a Wednesday. On this Wednesday Brother Henry and Sister Riley were leaving for Washington, DC, because the aliens were fake and had to be unmasked, and because Sister Riley's son Gabriel was the child of God. Truman repeated this to himself every so often, to keep it fresh. He came to the berm surrounding the Narrow Path Salvation Church early in the afternoon, and Sister Riley nodded at him as he came through the gate.

"We've been waiting for you, Truman," she said. "Gabriel's time is coming." Truman looked at the ground and followed her inside.

✦✦✦

"Brethren," began Brother Henry, "The Lord surely smiles on all of you for making the journey here. I know some of you — Brother Truman, some others — travel many hours to worship with us, and I appreciate your dedication to the Lord. We need that dedication now more than ever. Never has the world sunk nearer the abyss than at this moment, and never have you — each and every one of you — been so important to His work.

"The plan I'm about to discuss with you has been two long years in the making. At every step it has been opposed by the forces of evil, and if any of you don't believe in evil after what's happened these last two years then maybe you'd better leave right now."

No one moved, but Henry let that last sink in for a bit anyway. Then he walked to the back of the platform he stood on to preach and swept aside a hanging tapestry emblazoned with the words

WATCH, PREPARE, REJOICE, BEHOLD encircling the planet Earth. Behind the tapestry was a steel door pocked with large-caliber bullet dents like inverted pimples. Truman had helped Brother Henry and Brother Robert salvage it from the Rock Island Arsenal after the first Mississippi floods. Robert himself claimed he'd put the original pockmarks in the door, in a failed Patriot attack a dozen years ago.

"I have kept a secret from you, brethren," Brother Henry said, allowing an appropriate note of contrition to color his voice. "Not a secret for its own sake, but a secret that had to be kept until it could ripen. Well, now it has. The little mustard seed has grown into a mighty tree, and now is the time for us to reap what we have sown."

Henry unbolted the door and swung it open, revealing a concrete stairway lit by a single trouble light strung from the ceiling. Truman gasped as colors flickered at the edges of his vision. "Come with me, friends. It's time for all secrets to come out in the open," Brother Henry said.

The eleven members of the Narrow Path Salvation Church rose as one and stepped slowly toward the open doorway. Sister Riley was at the head of the group. Brother Henry led them down into a cramped basement, and waited for them all to assemble before he spoke again.

A fan whirred somewhere, stroking Truman's face with recycled air. He took a deep breath, watching as others did the same, and marveled at Brother Henry's secret. "For seven years, even before I understood what it was all for, I have been building in this room. As a young man, new to the calling of God, I heard a man say that the voice that is not heard beyond a single room might as well not speak at all; well, from this detritus I cobbled together an apparatus that would carry our voice from Moline to Marrakesh. And when the world sees what I mean for them to see..." Brother Henry paused. Truman wiped tears from his eyes. "Revelations spoke of not one false Messiah but many," Brother Henry went on, and Truman lost himself in wonder at what Brother Henry had done with the junk Truman had salvaged from the flooded-out Arsenal and the Bettendorf City Hall and the abandoned office buildings on the outskirts of the Quad Cities.

Tables sagged under the weight of receivers and transmitters, computer terminals and old tube television sets. Cables like the braids of a robot Rapunzel lay tangled in the corners and hung from ducts in the low ceiling. And in the middle of it all, the crowning achievement: a working satellite hookup, linked to a dish Truman and Brother Sam had dragged by horse from the Holiday Inn off the 280 bypass. "A voice crying in the wilderness I might be," Brother Henry, "but it'll sure as God's will be a loud voice.

"'In the beginning, God created the heaven and the earth,'" he quoted softly. Truman's lips moved with the words. Brother Henry made his way to the center of the room, to stand by the thick conduit that led out behind the church building, where the satellite sat waiting. "And He created the birds of the air and the fish of the sea, and all the creeping things. And, brethren, He created you and He created me. But does it say anywhere in the words of the Bible that God created aliens? That He created extraterrestrials? That He created two-legged monsters that smell like a drained swamp and look like a New Age cartoon fantasy?"

Brother Henry paused, and Sister Riley chimed in. "No, it doesn't," she said.

"That's right, LaWanda. It does not. The Creation story does not say that God created aliens. Now why do you suppose that is? Is it because God forgot to mention aliens? Is it because when He set down the catalog of all the glories of His Creation, He somehow didn't get around to the Bettys?" A few of the flock were shaking their heads. Truman shook his head too. "That's right; doesn't make much sense, does it? In fact, it doesn't make any sense at all that the Lord God Himself would forget to mention these so-called ETs. It doesn't make any sense that the Lord would set down a record of the beast Leviathan, which no man since Noah has ever laid eyes on, and have the Bettys slip His mind.

"So, friends, I have a question for you. Why would the Lord of all Creation give us a record of every animal and bird and creeping thing that doesn't include these aliens?" Again, Henry paused, and again Sister Riley's voice cut through the silence like Abraham's stone knife.

"Because they don't exist."

"Bless you, Sister LaWanda. They don't exist," Brother Henry repeated. "There are no aliens! There's no such thing as UFOs or little green men or Klingons, and there's no such thing as Bettys. Amen to that."

"Amen," the flock murmured.

"Now friends," Brother Henry continued, "I have another question for you. Have you heard anywhere else — from the government, from the television, from the intellectuals — that Bettys don't exist? No you haven't. Well, why not?

"Here's your answer, brothers and sisters: they don't want you to know. They are hiding the truth from you. Your government is hiding the truth, because ignorant people are easily led. Once we believe one lie, we'll believe another, and believe you me—once they've told one lie, they'll tell another. That, friends, is the Antichrist's bread and butter. If we start believing in lies, we fall prey to the Father of Lies.

"Ignorant people are easily led, and that baldheaded professor Waldrop thinks we are ignorant. He thinks that we won't ask questions, that we won't bother to discover the truth just like he expects us to believe that God didn't bother to mention the Bettys in His story of Creation. But we don't believe in a forgetful God, do we? And we don't believe in a government that lies to its people."

"Amen to that," said Sister Riley.

"That's right, amen." Brother Henry went to a table and picked up a sheet of paper. "And amen to this, too. This is our Constitution, brethren, the document our country is founded on. It says in here that when the government shall lose the confidence of the people, that they have the right to dissolve that government and raise a new one in its place. We have that right.

"But rights aren't any good if we don't exercise them, are they? If we don't exercise them, we are the ignorant people that our government thinks we are. Well, brethren," Brother Henry said, laying the paper back down, "I refuse to be ignorant. I refuse to ignore the call of duty spelled out in the Constitution of the United States of America. And according to our Constitution, we are duty-bound to act."

"Excuse me, Brother Till."

Brother Henry held out a hand towards big blond Brother Riley, standing in his green coveralls at the foot of the stairway. "Brother Earl. What's on your mind?"

Brother Riley scratched one of his jug ears and hesitated before speaking. "I've been listening,

Brother Till, and I'm all for what you say, but I've got a question. I guess...well, why would the government make up something like the Bettys? I mean, they ain't soldiers or cannibals, and they ain't stole our women. What's the use in making up something that doesn't do you no good?"

"Well, Brother Earl," Brother Henry said, "that's a good question. Let's think about it. Now before I said that ignorant people are easily led. You remember me saying that?"

"Sure."

"All right. It follows then, doesn't it, that the best way to lead people contrary to their best interests is to make them believe that they're ignorant. If you're Waldrop, you know that if you can make people believe that you know something they don't, they'll listen to whatever you have to say. One of the best ways to do that is to create a false enemy to distract people from the fact that you're the real problem. Nero did that with the early Church, didn't he? And the Romans didn't notice their Empire falling to ruin because watching Christian women torn to pieces by lions was more fun." Brother Henry waved behind him at the stacked video monitors against the wall. "More camera-friendly. More *telegenic*. And that, Brother Earl, is exactly what's happening here. Old Waldrop and his cronies think that if we don't know the Bettys aren't real, we'll be distracted from the real problem. Am I making sense?"

Brother Riley nodded, and Brother Henry continued. "And that isn't the worst of it, brethren," he said, jabbing a finger for emphasis. "The worst of it is how they've done it, the diabolical cleverness they've used to deceive us. You see, even if we don't believe in aliens, even if we think the Bettys are dressed-up humans in an evil masquerade, *we're still wrong.* The real truth is so much worse, so much more evil, that I tremble in my heart thinking of the Satanic mind that could conceive such a plan.

"The Bettys, friends, aren't aliens, but they aren't human either. What they are is the first wave of Satan's soldiers, *bioengineered* from humans who sold their souls to the Prince of Darkness in return for dominion over God's green earth. Why else would they be able to breathe our air? Why else would they be able to eat potatoes and green beans like any normal person? Because they were once human; now *science* has made them something else. Science has made them fallen angels, and they won't stop until they've made the rest of us just like them.

"The government may have created them, people, but remember Pandora's Box. Sometimes there's truth in old heathen stories, and old Waldrop is going to find out that his brand-new race of Satanic supermen have ideas of their own. Evil cannot stand the sight of beauty, brethren, cannot stand to be reminded of its own ugliness. If we do not act, we will find ourselves in line to have our beauty of God's likeness, our *souls,* engineered away by the science of Beelzebub himself. We will be made soulless and rendered hideous in the sight of the Lord."

"Well, that won't happen," Brother Riley said. The other members chimed in with a chorus of *Amen,* and then a silence fell, broken only by the fan's whirr.

"Brother Till," someone finally said, "what are we gonna do?"

"Now we're asking the right questions," Brother Henry answered. "Sermon's over. Now it's time to make a plan of our own, and I've got a few ideas. Sister LaWanda has been in touch with some people sympathetic to our cause, and I'll leave it up to her to tell you what we've found."

Sister Riley stayed where she was, letting attention come to her. "Thank you, Henry. Earl and I get plenty of visitors, living off the highway as we do. People don't travel much any more, but when they do they seem to come by our place for water, or directions, or just to talk to another person. And lots of those people are thinking along the same lines as we are.

"A month or so back," LaWanda continued, "three fellas stopped at our house wanting gasoline, of all things, as if we were the King of Siam and just had tanks of it in the garage."

"King of Siam," Brother Riley chortled. "As if."

Sister Riley shot him a glance and he quieted. "Well, we couldn't help them out with that, but while talking to them I got the impression that they were kindred spirits, if you know what I mean. We aren't the only ones who have thought about these aliens — God speaks to anyone who'll listen. I won't bore you with the whole story, but the upshot of it is there's going to be a meeting, arranged by these new friends of ours, and if we can get to that meeting we'll have a chance to get hold of one of those Bettys and unmask it for the world to see."

Brother Sam Platte spoke up, his reedy voice sparking numbers from behind Truman's eyeballs. "Sound like a trap to me. Who's to say your three friends weren't Fed spies, knowing we're about the Lord's work?"

"That's all been checked out, Sam," Brother Henry said. "Those men were part of — well, the media'd most likely call it a conspiracy, but I guess that's what the Romans said about the Apostles." A burst of nervous laughter drowned out the clattering of the fan.

"And you think we can just kidnap one of these Bettys and bring it back here? Brother Till,

Washington, DC's a thousand miles away. How're we gonna get there?"

"All taken care of," Brother Henry said. "Many of those who feel as we do aren't quite willing to take up arms themselves, but they're certainly not afraid to lend a hand to those who will."

"We have fuel stops set up all along the way," Sister Riley interjected. "In Chicago, Columbus...I don't remember all of them, but don't you worry. The Lord is bringing his soldiers together."

"Couldn't have said it better myself, Sister." Brother Henry went to the main monitor and switched it on. A battlefield scene appeared; gas-masked troops crouched in the downwash of an armored helicopter under a smoky sky.

"When we have that alien impostor unmasked," Brother Henry said, "we'll bounce its debased demonic image off every satellite in the sky. Man is made in the image of God, brethren, but we'll prove just how far away from our Maker's plan some of our fellow men have fallen."

On the screen, a journalist appeared in flak vest and army helmet. Behind him artillery explosions pocked a barren desert landscape.

Brother Henry returned his attention to his assembled flock. "Only four of us will be able to make the trip. We have to move fast, and we need to leave people behind so our church will be protected. I've prayed on this, brethren, and God has guided me. Brother Sam, Sister LaWanda and Brother Eric will come along. Each of the rest of you will have certain tasks while we're gone. Satan's troops are everywhere, we all know that, and we can be sure that they'll try whatever they can to destroy everything we've built. So we'll defend ourselves against them. You've all armed yourselves?"

Everyone nodded. Several of the flock patted holsters or made reflexive gestures toward vest pockets.

"Good," Henry said. "I'll ask that three of you are here at all times, in addition to Brother Truman, who I would like to deputize in my absence. Brother Truman, would you mind staying here full-time until we return?"

Truman heard his name, but he was watching the numbers go through the wires of a broken radio. "Brother Truman?"

"I will," Truman said.

"Thank you, Brother," Brother Henry said.

"I don't need to go home," Truman said.

"You other seven," Henry said, "Robert, Ginny, David, Morris, Tim, Rhonda, Earl. Keep us in your prayers, and we'll do likewise. I don't want you to feel left out, now; remember that even if we succeed in Washington, DC — and we will, because God is with us — it won't matter unless we can come back to a living house of God here." He searched their faces for signs of resentment, and found none.

"Now it's time to be about the Lord's work," Henry finished. "Gird yourselves, and let's be on the road."

✦✦✦

Truman sat in the dark, the ventilator's oscillating rattle making him think about time. Visualizing time as a clockspring, circular, circular, circular, but unwinding to a point. Even now that was happening. Things were winding down to the point when time would reveal itself to have never existed. A digital clock in the War Room counted on — 1:16:44, 1:16:45, 1:16:46 — and Truman smiled at it, remembering a day before the earthquakes, before Vision. Bicycle Time. When he'd read something in a book. We measure time, the book had said, because we have conceived of time as something that can be measured. Truman hadn't believed the book then, but the Visions had revealed many things and now he saw what the book had been trying to say. Time wasn't one facet of experience; it *was* experience, it engulfed experience. Clocks are like maps, Truman thought. They try to represent what can only be known.

That was one of his secrets. He knew that the clock Brother Till had set up on the counter was measuring human experience. It had nothing to do with time, could have nothing to do with real time. Real time held itself apart from experience.

Real time was the mind of God.

Clocks counted like idiot children, making lines of numbers the way maps made bright lines out of invisible borders that people would kill for. All lies, waiting to be revealed when the clockspring at last relaxed and time became known as something that had never been.

Truman pinched himself lest the thickets of vision catch his horns and leave him vulnerable to the hooked knife of human misunderstanding. Brother Till had been gone a day; the sun had come and gone again. But Truman had not left the War Room. Upstairs David and Rhonda and whoever else came and went, trading places with guns and sharp eyes and angry prayer. They came to check on him, but he forgot their names and they went away without speaking, leaving him alone in the War Room with the clattering fan and the idiot clock spinning bright numbers that meant less than words.

He pinched himself again, raising a welt on the inside of his arm. The Second Vision was coming, he felt its onset like a fever, but until it came he had to be able to live like a human, had to be able to participate in time and conversation. Soon all that would change, but not quite yet. Everything could not yet soften into allegory.

Something had made him pinch himself. A noise from upstairs? He struggled out of his mind and listened.

Shouts, from outside. Loud voices shrill with fear. Gunshots.

Was it April 19th already? Brother Till always held a pageant called Slaughter of the Innocents on Waco Day. Once, when the Last Times had still been only prophecy, he'd even taken the pilgrimage to the holy site. Truman hadn't been in the church then; that had been during Bicycle Time.

More gunshots and Brother David, bellowing like a bull, his voice distorted coming through heating ducts, unleashing a torrent of curses in the name of God. Truman ran to the stairs and took them three at a time, feeling some of the old strength still in his thighs. He reached the steel door in five steps and was about to shove it open when a burst of automatic gunfire slammed into the door, raising a new line of bumps that ran from left to right at waist level.

The impact numbed Truman's hands. He stepped back, feeling his heel slip on the edge of the top stair. His hands looked the same, except for the one finger that was bent strangely to the side, but he couldn't feel them at all. If he'd been one step faster, or had thought a moment less…

God watched over His prophets. John the Baptist had lived on locusts and honey; lions had not touched Daniel. And bullets had not touched Truman Throckmorton.

Thank you, he thought. This was not Vision, but it was a sign. God had not forgotten him. *Thank you,*

Lord. Had my faith weakened without me knowing it? Now I am ready again, ready to be Your Vessel. Take me and fill me and pour me out into the souls of this wasteland.

The gunfire and shouting grew sporadic, then several silent minutes passed. Pain began to swell in Truman's hands and he moaned quietly, clenching his teeth against the sound. Who had attacked the church? CAP2 radicals? Or had it been — was it — the Arabs coming down from Detroit?

It could be anyone, Truman realized. And when they had taken what they wanted, they would burn the Narrow Path Salvation Church to the ground. With him in it, if he didn't do something.

God loved him, but having already stopped bullets, would the Father save him from fire as well? He helps those who help themselves, Truman thought. And I am not Shadrach, nor Meshach nor Abednego.

He could move his fingers a little, even though every twitch sent fresh jolts of pain all the way up to his shoulders. The hatch kept slipping from his numbed grip, but finally Truman spun it loose and leaned his weight into the battered door. It opened less than a foot before jamming; Truman squeezed awkwardly through the opening, holding his hands away from his sides.

Two steps into the sanctuary, he saw that the door had jammed against Brother David's body. A rifle lay near Brother David's head, part of its stock blown away. Blood stained the exposed wood and soaked from four holes in the back of Brother David's denim shirt. The bullets that had hit the door had torn through Brother David first, Truman realized; he had died defending the War Room.

And defending me, he thought.

Whoever had killed Brother David had gone, though; the sanctuary was empty. Truman stepped off the dais and walked up the aisle between the rows of chairs. Shell casings clinked under his feet and he could see bullet holes pocking the sanctuary walls. Where were the others, Rhonda and — what was his name — Morris? Dead, or taken prisoner? Escaped, maybe? Why hadn't the invaders pushed into the War Room?

"Freeze it, fundy," a harsh voice snapped. Truman stopped in his tracks as a man dressed all in black stepped out of Brother Henry's office at the side of the sanctuary. He held a rifle leveled at Truman's midsection.

This is the man who killed Brother David, Truman thought. He pointed his gun just like that and bullets ripped through Brother David into the War Room door.

"Who are you?" he said softly.

"You Truman Throckmorton?" The man stepped closer to Truman, and Truman realized that he was Chinese. Suddenly everything made sense.

"I — I am a servant of God."

"Aren't we all," the Chinese said.

"His prophet."

The Chinese sighed. "Well, come on, prophet. I've got a little revelation for you."

I thought all of the Chinese had moved to San Francisco, Truman mused, with the homosexuals and environmentalists. He felt detached from what was going on, even though God had recently saved his life. A feeling of protection, of divine benison, suffused him and kept him from panicking. Seems to me, he thought, that all the Chinese lived in San Francisco now. Like all the Arabs in Detroit. An image of endless columns of marching Chinese, spreading out from California into the heartland, swam in Truman's head — the thousand million of Revelation, meeting a kaffiyehed horde of Arabs at the Mississippi River. The first shots of the Battle of Armageddon had been fired, here at the Narrow Path Salvation Church. *And I am left alone to tell thee.*

But tell who? *David, your reward will be in Heaven.*

The Chinese hustled Truman out through the front door and past a group of men with guns, standing in a half-circle around Sister Rhonda and Brother Morris. Brother Morris' arms hung at his sides, and blood dripped from his fingers. He had tears in his eyes. Sister Rhonda's face was turned away.

Dead so that I might live, Truman thought. Why am I so important? Why, Lord? One of the men called out to the Chinese, but Truman didn't hear what he said and the Chinese led Truman around the corner of the building. A burst of rude laughter followed them, and a crackling burst of gunfire shot into the air.

It was dark behind the church building, but the night was clear and the moon was nearly full. Truman only stumbled once before the Chinese brought him to a halt. His head was spinning from the pain in his finger; it reminded him strangely of an example written on the blackboard in freshman geometry, back in Bicycle Time. His finger was obtuse.

And so was he, worrying about being burned alive when the real worry was right in front of him. What did the Chinese want? Why had he come from California looking for Truman? How did he know who Truman was?

Just like the Romans, Truman thought. Sooner or later they came armed looking for the faithful.

He looked up at the Chinese, who was speaking to him. "Your finger hurt?"

Truman nodded.

"Hold out your hand."

So now I'll be tortured, Truman thought. There was nowhere to run. He steeled himself with the memory of saints, and his lips started moving before he'd thought what to say. "The Lord is my shepherd, I shall not want…" he whispered. There was strength in the words, and he held out his hand.

The Chinese grasped Truman's wrist in his left hand and ran the fingers of his right along Truman's bent finger.

"…he makes me lie down in green pastures…" Truman closed his eyes, hid behind the words.

The grip on his wrist tightened, and a nauseating bolt of pain shot from his finger as the Chinese gave it a sharp jerk. Sweat broke out on Truman's face. The words failed him for a moment, but he recovered: "…the valley of the shadow of Death…" He trailed off as the Chinese let go of his wrist.

"You can open your eyes," the Chinese said. "We need to talk."

"I don't want to talk to you," Truman answered, his eyes still shut. "I'm a Christian."

"I could care less. Open your eyes."

Truman did, and saw that his finger was now straight. The damaged joint was swelling, though, and starting to darken even in the dim light.

"What's your name?" he said, to say something.

The Chinese frowned. "Lucky," he said after a pause.

"Why'd you kill Brother David?"

"Best thing that ever happened to him. A guy like that, his aim in life is to go out in a blaze of glory."

"Your name is really Lucky?"

"Sure is," Lucky said.

"That's not a Chinese name."

"I'm not Chinese," Lucky said patiently. "I'm Laotian. But we need to talk about something else. Pay attention now."

Sister Rhonda screamed out front. "Who are you?" Truman asked. "Are you meeting the Arabs from Detroit?"

Lucky started to say something, then checked himself. He pulled an envelope from his coat pocket. "There's bad shit going on out front, Truman. I don't like it, but sometimes you have to take the long view. Sit down, okay?"

Truman sat in the gravel under the building's rain gutter. The pain in his finger was settling into a steady throb; he set his hand carefully in his lap.

Lucky — if that was his name — handed Truman a duffel bag. "You're going to be traveling soon, Truman."

"I knew it," Truman said.

"Right." Lucky was digging in his coat pocket. "Make sure you take this wherever you go. There's a million dollars in it. You hear me?"

"Yes," Truman said. A million dollars. What for? He took the duffel and ran his arms through the straps, wearing it like a backpack. Lucky switched on a flashlight. "Look at this, Truman," he said, holding something in the light.

Truman caught a glimpse of a picture, a black man with a gap-toothed smile and tangled hair, before everything in his field of vision fragmented and blew away into a swirl of fractal chaos.

Vision, Truman thought, or didn't think: Vision like a bullet tore open his mind and somersaulted between thoughts he tried to form. *At play in the field of Vision.* The words broke up into numbers in his head, and the numbers took on shape and color as his body spasmed, banging his head into the wall.

Lying on his back, he reached up to cover his eyes against the fearful brilliance of the colors; a second spasm struck him and he punched himself in the cheek. Fresh waves of pain exploded from his finger, then turned the color of numbers which was the color of the mind of God. Gunshots boomed somewhere like drums relaying the Gospel across trackless jungle. The jungle was Truman's mind, and every tree was a color, and every bird and insect feeding from the trees was a word that tingled like an earthquake heralding the footsteps of God.

God stood before Truman, made of numbers and time. God stood before Truman, a digital clock counting backwards. 1:16:46, 1:16:45, 1:16:44…

ARISE, TRUMAN, God said, and his words ate at Truman's weeping mind like insects, burrowing and nesting in the prismatic jungle. ARISE, AND GO INTO THE CITY, AND IT SHALL BE TOLD THEE WHAT THOU MUST DO.

ARISE, and the clock counted backwards.

✦✦✦

Strange lights flared under the water around the ruin of the Rock Island Arsenal, only they didn't reflect on the bridge's rusting girders and Truman wasn't entirely sure they were lights. He stumbled across the bridge, too sensitive to the way the world moved around him, too sensitive and afraid that the next rotation might throw him off course, turn him from the Path into the wilderness. Over his head, angels were skywriting in invisible ink, writing out his itinerary. RUN ALL THE WAY TO THE WALLED CITY, the Chinese had said, or had that been the voice of God? Truman cried out from fear and uncertainty.

New York. A thousand miles.

But what is a thousand miles to me? he thought, fear swept away by the wind of revelation. Or a thousand years, now that I have Vision?

He reached his house and charged panting up the stairs, stumbling in through the open door of his room. One strap of the duffel bag caught on his doorknob and spun him around. He fell onto his right side and stayed there, facing the clock that had fallen from the wall, so long ago it seemed. Truman heaved like a man rescued from drowning, exalted in exhaustion and holy madness. Oh yes, he thought. But the madness of prophets, madness of numbers, madness of 1:16:46, 1:16:45, 1:16:44…

"The Mind of God," he breathed, and outside the words wrote themselves across the naked sky. Angels erased them and wrote GO in shapes and numbers.

"Yes, right, go, I will." New York, a thousand miles, and not a moment to spare. The Chinese had let him go for a reason, whether by the hand of God or through some plan of his own. Either way, the time had come, Truman realized, to pour himself out into the thirsty souls of the Last Times. The day and the hour, hidden so long, come round at long last. Lucky, Truman thought. He's not Lucky, I am. Not Chinese. Lucky lucky lucky. Truman lurched to his feet, already feeling his strength coming back, and went into his bedroom thinking Circles. More circles, I will use circles, everything has come full circle. The numbers in his head counted circles, he spoke circles aloud and the angels erased them.

In the corner, leaning against the cracked plaster wall, was his bicycle. Its name was the name of the donkey that Christ rode into Jerusalem. Its name was a journey across empty farms and cities eating themselves alive. Circles; Bicycle Time was now. All time was Bicycle Time. The bicycle was the words of a forgotten prophet, waiting for time and Vision to reclaim it. Truman crushed his cap down on his head, found his riding glasses in the dresser, changed out of soiled khaki into spandex unfolding brightly from the drawer that always stuck when he opened it. Once, in Bicycle Time, he had ridden 200 miles in a day. But that would not be fast enough now.

Quickly he gathered what he would need: batteries for his headlight, pump for old tires, toolkit fallen from its peg on the wall. Water bottles.

DON'T WORRY ABOUT FOOD, the angels wrote. CONSIDER THE LILIES OF THE FIELD.

So I will eat sunshine and wind, Truman thought. Locusts and honey. I will eat the lilies of the field and feel the number of us grow toward the color of one.

Angels wrote directions in the sky as Truman pedaled east toward the moon, mile markers his guides.

✦✦✦

Warm morning sunlight gleamed on New York's skyscrapers as Truman pedaled up to the toll booths on the New Jersey side of the George Washington Bridge. Lights over each lane blinked from red to green and back again. In bright cirrus whispers, the angels, hidden by daylight, told him what the lights said.

"All right then," he answered, coasting to a halt and dropping his bicycle against the guardrail. He walked along a line of tractor-trailers, looking out across the river at the city of God, walled like Jericho before Joshua's trumpet. As he passed the booths he began to run, the attendants' shouts reaching him only as numbers: 1:16:46, 1:16:45, 1:16:44...

So little time. He'd covered a thousand miles in four days, eating only his own hair (EVEN THE HAIRS OF YOUR HEAD ARE NUMBERED, the angels had mentioned, and Truman had wanted all of those numbers inside him) and sleeping not at all. Even so, he burned with energy, felt strength in his legs and lungs as he reached the top of the bridge's shallow arc and accelerated down the incline. He hit the New York side at a dead run and did not slow down until the angels told him to turn south on Riverside Drive. They guided him through throngs of people with numbers for faces who shouted shapes, breathed out the stink of time.

Relax, said the angels. *You're almost there. Relax and breathe, Truman. Pour yourself out on these maddened throngs desperate for salvation.*

"I am Your Vessel, Lord," Truman panted. "Broken into shivers." Walking was harder than running. He leaned to his right as he went, struggling to keep his balance with everything so slow and close. Someone stopped him and shouted shapes into his face; Truman breathed in the shapes and exhaled his answer. "All time is Bicycle Time," he told the man. "Ask the angels if I can eat sunlight."

The man stepped back, leaving a hole in time that Truman plunged through, running again, feeling the giant spring in the spine of the universe slacken with every step he took.

✦✦✦

Inside finally, after four days of wind and merciless sun. Hidden from the sky, but the angels still fed him information through the steady flame of a candle, flickering in the darkness ahead. Truman walked with his hands brushing either wall of the corridor, his eyes fastened on the flame. Flickering; moving air. Just me, turning with the clockspring earth? Or—

Simultaneously, both hands found gaps in the corridor's walls. Which way? Right, he decided; I've been leaning that way anyway, ha ha. His feet found stairs, counted them as he descended. Eight steps, right turn; eight more, right turn. Back the way he'd started, under the flooded street. Confident, Truman strode through the absolute blackness, hearing a trickle of water somewhere. Was he under the river now? A ghost of breeze touched his face and he stopped. Put a foot carefully out, found another stair.

How a blind man walks, thought Truman. He went down the stairs as the afterimage of the candle's flame danced into patters behind his eyes. Holy blindness, when the eyes made their own light. 1:16:46, 1:16:45, 1:16:44, each step a tick on the clock counting down to Bicycle Time.

At the fifth step he splashed. How far did the water go, and how deep? There will only be eight steps, he thought, and three more splashes proved him right. Waist-deep in the river, Truman kept walking until the patterns behind his eyes were blotted out by real light.

He stepped up into a cinder-block room the size of the church sanctuary. "Had to take the back way," he said, and giggled as he stumbled to his right on the top step. "Geometry, rotation. Can't be denied."

Five men—no, three plus two, men and angels— leaped up from the card table they'd been sitting around, knocking over folding chairs and reaching for guns. They stepped back as Truman wobbled up to the table, fascinated by the patterns the cards made. Symmetry from randomness—proof of God. What more did the mind need?

Over the sound of dripping water, one of the men said, "Merciful Jesus, it's him."

"Truman," another said, and Truman's head snapped up. The man had a joker's face, but where was his cap? "Truman, have you seen Gabriel Riley?"

A broad grin split Truman's sunburnt lips. "Gabriel Riley," he said, tasting sudden blood in his mouth. "You know him too. I am the Vessel, poured out upon the waters. Broken into shivers."

"I think we'd better get the fuck out of here," someone said.

"Watch your language, please," said the angels, but they followed the men out through a metal door—circle inside a square—looking nervously over their shoulders before the door clanged shut and Truman was alone. He took a seat at the table and waited. Falling water splashed numbers into his mind, and counted the patterns the cards used his hands to create.

✦ ✦ ✦

Truman looked up as Gabriel Riley approached the table. Riley looked sad. Jesus had always looked sad. "Cards are all about time," Truman said in a husky whisper. "They're teaching me time."

"Yeah," Riley said. He sat in the chair opposite Truman. "Maybe you could teach me."

Truman looked at him doubtfully. "I guess. Maybe." He brightened suddenly. "Sure. Probabilities. Do you know Go Fish?"

"I only play Go Fish for big stakes," Riley said. He laid something on the table. A gun like the one Lucky the Chinese had.

"Big stakes," Truman repeated. "Your mother told me you'd be here. Lucky the Chinese said I had a million dollars for you, but I forgot it somewhere. Million million million," he said, and his eyes drifted shut.

Riley smiled. "That's okay."

Truman opened his eyes again. "I am the Vessel, poured out upon the waters. My stakes are the biggest." He gathered up the cards. "Three, two, one," he said. "That's it, you know. After that, there's nothing. All time is Bicycle Time."

"Why don't I deal the first one?" Riley said.

Nate

ate Drinkwater was trying simultaneously to shield his match from the rain and avoid stepping in one of the deepening puddles on the sidewalk when he noticed the commotion in the alley behind Grand Entrail Station. He tried to look out of the corner of his eye without seeming obvious, but all he could see in the dark was a vast afterimage of the flaring match. The match was his last; he stopped and applied all his concentration to lighting his bent cigarette, hoping that P.K. would have more down at Joe Mud's. The cigarette finally caught and Nate dropped the match into the streaming gutter, blinking as the afterimage faded. He slipped around the corner of an old brick warehouse and peered down the alley.

This part of town might as well have been on the moon for all it had in common with the nonstop wired infohype of Wall Street or the other Claimed precincts. Down this close to the dikes, it was still possible to duck underneath the gaze of City Hall and the curious peering of the Bettys. The slipstream of the bitstream, Nate thought.

It was dark here in the dikes' shadow, as if the
light had been crushed under the noise of the pumps
and the weight of the East River. The only light came
from the security fixture over the Station's delivery
door, a flat orange glare diffused by the pounding
rain. Three men stood below one corner of the loading
dock, and from the looks of it one of them was in
bad trouble. It was hard to tell for sure in the
downpour, and the match's fading purple afterimage
still clouded Nate's vision, but—oh shit—there it was.
A flash of reflected sodium-arc, three times quick,
and then the killer flipped the blade into a Dumpster
and sauntered off down the alley with his companion.
The dead man crumpled to the concrete without so
much as a wheeze.

It was odd. Slip a blade into somebody right
behind an organ bank and not even try to sell the
corpse; what kind of sense did that make? Nate shook
his head as he counted backwards from twenty. When
nobody else came down the alley, he flicked away
the drowned cigarette and tiptoed around the
puddles to the body.

The dead man was in shirtsleeves, and one thing
was apparent right away. Whoever had done this guy
hadn't cared whether they could sell him or not; the
three stab wounds were close together under the left
armpit, looking like ragged gill slits. Left lung was
shredded, and most likely the heart too. Nate
scratched at his receding hairline and water dripped
from his hatbrim up the sleeve of his raincoat. It had
to be a hit, and that meant that he should turn and
march straight out of the alley, out of the
neighborhood in fact, and be glad that neither killer
had seen him.

Twenty years ago, I might have thought this was
a thrill, Nate thought nervously, watching the rain

fall on the dead man's upturned face. The corpse wore the pinched expression that Nate had always associated with getting a shot. A steady rivulet of rainwater ran from the crow's-feet at the corner of one eye and pooled in the seashell curve of his ear. *Water on the brain,* Nate thought. He suppressed an urge to giggle, then looked around again. What the hell.

He squatted next to the dead man and patted his pockets, coming up with a keyring, two quarters, a business card, and a real leather wallet bulging with cash. Nate stuffed the cash into his coat pocket without counting it, then pitched the wallet and the keyring into the Dumpster. He shook the two quarters in his palm as he stood up and read the card.

W. L. ASCHENBRENNER, it said. KAPLAN, NG, ASCHENBRENNER AND NG, ATTORNEYS AT LAW. Voice and vid information followed, and a Washington, DC, street address.

"DC?" Nate said aloud. Not many possible lawyers with walletsful of cash went wandering down back alleys in this neighborhood at two-thirty in the morning. Something was not kosher here. He flipped the card over and noticed something scrawled on the back. ORACLE ON 34TH STREET.

Weirder and weirder. What would a DC lawyer want with the Oracle, if the dead man actually went with the name on the card? Nate looked at the corpse again; the face seemed awfully young to be an established lawyer in a piranha town like DC, and the flattop haircut wasn't exactly lawyer chic. Nate was suddenly annoyed with himself for tossing the wallet immediately into the Dumpster; now his curiosity wouldn't let him leave without digging it out.

A clattering farther down the alley brought Nate to his feet. He didn't want to be caught at a murder scene; New York City cops had lost the remnants of their sense of humor since the Murray Hill riots last March. He slipped the card into his pocket next to the wad of cash and hurried back onto the street, the two quarters held tightly in his right hand.

✦✦✦

P.K. Fizer was exactly where Nate expected him to be, babbling to strangers at the back corner table across from the door labeled EMPLOYEES ONLY. At this hour, the sole denizens of Joe Mud's Cafe were insomniacs and streeties. P.K., like many other regulars, received his paper mail care of Joe Mud's, and he kept all of his books stacked behind the counter under trays of aluminum teapots. He had a day job with the New York Bureau of Education and Corrections, but what he really did was sit in Joe Mud's fomenting revolution. And he did his best to look the part of revolutionary genius, rarely changing his clothes or combing his wooly tangle of red hair. The lenses of his wire-rimmed glasses were often opaque with fingerprints and dust, and even his goatee usually managed to look disreputable, bristling like an orange sea urchin from his lower lip. His laptop, covered in bumper-sticker slogans, was open on the table in front of him; it was old enough that most newer micros couldn't even talk to it, which was why P.K. liked it.

Nate liked P.K. in spite of his pomposity, because he'd once been the same kind of nutty-professor polymath himself. But there was little room for an educated humanist in twenty-first century New York, and over the years Nate had been reduced to a part-time reference job at the print desk of the NYPL. Right now P.K. was waving a much-scribbled-on sheet of paper in the air as he exclaimed, "One tractor trailer full of scrap iron and concrete, whatever, going seventy or eighty miles an hour at the right point, my friend, and whoosh! Lower Manhattan becomes a cesspool for real instead of just metaphorically." He slapped the paper onto the table with a flourish.

"Damn," the man across from P.K. said. He was a tremendous shaven-headed slab, three hundred hairless pounds of stoned potential mishap. His eyes were wide and darkly bloodshot, the irises barely visible ringing bottomless full-moon pupils. He cupped a mug between massive hands, nervously picking scabs from knuckles tattooed with bullseyes. A similar tattoo fluoresced on the crown of his skull, crosscut by a thick angular scar.

Slumming rich kid, Nate thought, noting the dual jacks behind the baldy's right ear.

"That's all it would take?" The baldy tore loose a scab, flicked it onto the floor. "Damn."

"Well, it depends on where you hit, but yeah. That's all. Glub glub."

"But shit, you'd have to be crazy," the baldy objected. "If you drove the truck, you'd be the first to go."

"What a way to go, though, eh? Hello, history!" P.K. was clearly enjoying himself. Scheming was his element. Throwing bombs of language because he didn't have any of the real kind. Nate thought he was nuts.

"*You're* fuckin' crazy," the baldy said. He stood suddenly and Nate backed a judicious distance towards the door. "I just said it'd be nova cool to flood the place; I don't have no *agenda* or nothin'." He shook his head. "Outta your goddamn mind. I look like I wanna die to you?"

The baldy shambled towards the door. "Whoosh," he said as he pushed out into the rain.

He was briefly visible as a shadow on the other side of the scarred windows, silhouetted between a Mona Lisa bas-relief carved into the Plexiglas and the words CHUCK IS ON THE HILL spraypainted in a fading neon green.

Nate waited for him to pass, then sat down opposite P.K. "You sure know how to bring out the best in people," he said.

"You know, a bomb would work just as well," P.K. said by way of reply. "Also would remove the suicide element, if that wasn't attractive."

"Taking up terrorism now?"

"I never shy away from an interesting discussion, Nathan, and there are times when this...endless intellectualizing, though God knows I'm good at it, gets tiresome. Direct action appeals more and more." P.K. drained the last of his coffee. "Perhaps I've just become jaded at a young age."

Nate shook a smoke from a pack on the table. "You're gonna blow the dike," he said, in the tone of voice of a reporter confirming a fact he can't bring himself to take seriously.

P.K. didn't answer directly. "Has nobody informed you, Mr. Marlowe, that slouch hats have been passé for nearly eighty years?" he said.

"Eye of the beholder, my friend." Nate took off his hat and hung it on an empty chair. "Riddle me this, P.K.; a guy gets a knife stuck in him behind Grand Entrail Station, right by their delivery door. Two guys who did it don't try to sell him for parts, don't even take his cash. He's maybe thirty, no more, and he has this in his wallet." He discreetly showed P.K. the wad of bills.

P.K. chewed his lower lip. "Got to be a hit, right? Was he a courier?"

Nate shook his head. "Don't think so. He also had this." He handed P.K. the business card. P.K.

lifted an eyebrow as he read it, lifted the other when he saw what was written on the other side.

"Is the dead man this Aschenbrenner?" he asked. Nate shrugged. "Well, where's his wallet?"

"Still in the Dumpster," Nate said. "I didn't feel like taking the time to fish it out."

"Wait a minute," P.K. said. "They threw his wallet in the Dumpster but left his cash out?"

"Well, actually —"

"Let me guess. You grabbed the cash and pitched the wallet into the Dumpster, then wanted to know the identity of the deceased but not badly enough to go digging for it. Correct?" Nate nodded.

"Ah, Nathan," P.K. said ruefully. "Well, there's only one thing to do that I can see."

Nate was already shaking his head. "No. I don't want to go digging in the Dumpster behind Grand Entrail Station of all places, I'll probably get cholera or some forgotten jungle plague. It'll stink. The place will be crawling with cops. That baldy was right, you're crazy."

P.K. was looking quizzically at him. Nate paused.

"What the hell are you talking about, Nathan? Why would you want to go digging in a pile of discarded appendixes and eyelids when there's a much simpler path to the same objective?"

Nate shrugged; he could just go home and be happy with the found cash.

P.K. leaped from his chair, shut his laptop and quickly stashed it behind the counter. "Come on," he said.

"What are we doing?" Nate was suspicious. He still hadn't finished his smoke or wangled a cup of coffee.

"We'll consult the Oracle," P.K. said, "and find out if she was expecting Aschenbrenner or someone else." He looked Nate up and down, frowning. "You don't look much like a lawyer, but I guess you'll have to do. Comb your hair or something. Yeah, sweep it over the bald spot; that looks judicial."

P.K. offered Nate the business card, and Nate reluctantly took it. "No way this works," Nate said.

"We won't find out standing here," P.K. replied. He handed Nate his hat and pushed him towards the door.

✦✦✦

The Oracle was not actually on 34th Street, but as P.K. was fond of saying, even genuine fonts of wisdom are not disdainful of publicity. Its sooty brick facade was recessed between two abandoned storefronts near the end of what had once been a one-way ramp onto West Side Highway. That had been before sea level rose fifty feet and West Side Highway became the West Side Tunnel beneath the Hudson River Dike, and now the narrow street sloped gently down to dead end against graffitoed concrete. No sign advertised the Oracle's presence, and no light showed through the broken windows.

The dikes were not well maintained here; Nate and P.K. found themselves slogging knee-deep in chill, silted water by the time they approached the Oracle's front door. It was dark enough to see reflected stars wobbling and then disappearing in the ripples of their passage, even darker in the shadowed doorway. P.K. pushed the door open and peered in. He stepped inside. Nate started to follow, but P.K. motioned him back and disappeared into the building, the door creaking shut behind him.

Wonderful, Nate thought. Here I am, two o'clock in the goddamn morning, standing knee-deep in the

Hudson River posing as a dead lawyer from Washington, DC. What could be better? He stood for several minutes, watching the reflected stars resolve out of the chaos of ripples and cursing whatever Fates had introduced him to P.K. Fizer.

The door groaned open again, making Nate jump. P.K.'s head poked out. "Gave 'em the old Rosicrucian high sign," he said, and winked.

"The what?"

"Never mind. Just come on; they won't wait all night." Nate followed him inside and the door banged shut on the rippling reflected starlight.

✦✦✦

A candle flickered ahead of them, but it didn't throw nearly enough light to illuminate even a single wall. "You have to walk three steps toward it," P.K. whispered, "then feel for a stair going down."

Nate's fear sublimated into annoyance. "Jesus," he grumbled. "Spare me the Gothic bullshit."

"Nathan, you have no sense of occasion. This is an oracle, not a grocery store. Ah; here's the step. Careful."

They went down perhaps two dozen stairs, turning left after eight and again after sixteen. At the bottom of the stairway was a low passage. "I'm pretty sure this opens out into the subways somewhere," P.K. said, ducking under a pipe. "But I think it might be unfortunate to be sneaking around in this area."

"You would be right," a voice said from their left, and a powerful flashlight beam hit Nate squarely in the face. He flinched away from it and cracked his head into the wall, losing his balance. A hand grabbed his collar and pushed him in the direction of the flashlight. "Unscheduled detour, gents," said the voice. "The Oracle has no time for you tonight."

Nate struggled, twisting around to grab his captor's wrist. A bony knee slammed into his tailbone; his legs buckled and he choked back a surge of nausea. He let go, dizzied by the pain, and caught an odd fish-and-pine-needle smell.

People didn't smell like that. Bettys did.

Nate was shoved again in the direction of the light. He stumbled forward on rubbery legs, his eyes watering from the pain in the small of his back, following the bobbing beam as best he could.

✦✦✦

I'm in the Hall of the Goblin King, Nate thought. There go the ponies, and even if I get out, Gollum awaits.

The arched subterranean chamber looked as if it might once have been some kind of subway junction, but which one? For all Nate knew, they might have been under the river. The sound of falling water provided an eerie backdrop to the echo of his and P.K.'s footsteps as they were marched across a concrete platform and down a narrow stairway.

"I hope you guys's pumps don't fail," he said nervously.

"Please be silent," the Betty behind him hissed, and hit Nate on the back of the head for emphasis.

Nate couldn't see P.K., but he could hear his friend stumbling along behind him, wheezing as the damp air brought on his asthma. At the bottom of the stair, several inches of chilly water sloshed against a bolted steel door. Nate's guard clicked off his flashlight and banged on the door.

Wish I could see him, Nate thought. Way he smells, he's got to be a Betty, but Christ, I wish I could see him just to be sure.

As if it made any real difference to the situation.

There was a clank in the darkness, and a faint beam of light shone through an eye-level portal in the door. Then the light was blocked as someone on the other side pressed against the hole.

"Who goes?" a whiny voice asked, and Nate thought *Now I'm in a Prohibition speakeasy. The guy on the other side is probably six-nine and nicknamed Tiny.*

"Chickens coming home," said another voice. The guy holding P.K.? "Open up the roost."

Another clank and the door grated open, swinging into a dimly lit room about the size of Joe Mud's. Four men—humans, wearing what looked like black Army fatigues—sat around a folding table playing cards. The air in the room was thick with cigarette smoke, sweat and the odd pungency of Bettys.

Oh my God, I was right, Nate thought. It's a gangster movie, only with aliens.

The doorman wasn't what Nate had envisioned. He—or it—was, in fact, a Betty, also dressed in fatigues instead of the silky tunics they usually wore.

"Praise God you've returned," the Betty said. "Bring them in."

As Nate and P.K. stepped up out of the water into the room, one of the men at the table stood and approached P.K. He was taller than Nate, with a baby-fat-rounded face and wide blue eyes that, coupled with his turn-of-the-century haircut, made him the poster boy for a generation of student body presidents. Attached to his left breast pocket was a nameplate that read FISKE. "Are you the one who found the body?" he asked.

"Him," P.K. answered, inclining his head at Nate. They exchanged a quick glance, and Nate could see P.K. thinking *paramilitary fundamentalist Bettys?*

"Okay, you," Fiske said to Nate. "We need to talk."

"Look, I didn't kill the guy," Nate began, but Fiske cut him off.

"I know," he said. "I did. But that isn't important. What is important is that you came along and helped yourself to what was in his pockets."

"Oh shit," Nate said. "You can have it back. All of it. I didn't spend it." He caught himself wondering where his body would wash up, or whether they would encase him in concrete and build him into the base of a bus-station kiosk.

"Doesn't matter. We don't mind that you kept what you found. Shows you have sense. If you hadn't, the boys at the organ bank would've. Thing is, though, other people wouldn't see it the same way. Witnesses," Fiske indicated the three men still at the card table, "can place you in the neighborhood of the body very near the time of death. The decedent was what you might call an important person, and the police might be interested in talking to you."

Nate started to answer, but his throat had dried shut. Fiske went on.

"Now we don't want you to think of this as a threat," he said. "More like you returning a favor. After all, you did generate some revenue from the dear departed."

Nate turned to P.K., not sure what he wanted so say but hoping for a shot of P.K.'s manic cheer, and saw that he was now alone in the room with four humans and two Bettys. "Oh shit," he said again.

"He had someplace to go," Fiske said. "And you do too." He went to the table, beckoning Nate to follow.

"Ever been to Washington, DC?" Fiske shook a cigarette from a standard-issue military pack and lit it.

"Um, yeah. When I was a kid. Can I have one of those?"

"Sure. School trip?" Fiske lit Nate's cigarette and dropped the match into a puddle under the table.

"Sixth grade. 1997." Nate inhaled, felt the pure military-grade tobacco smooth him out a bit. I might just live through the night, he thought.

"Yeah, me too. Later, though, just when the floods started to get real bad."

"Fucking rich kids," one of the other men said.

The Bettys stepped up and, in unison, slapped the back of his head. "Watch your language, please," they said before returning to their position by the door.

"Rich, heck," Fiske said. "I sold hologrammed keychains for weeks. What's your name, man?"

"Me? Nate," Nate said.

"Nate what?"

"Nate Drinkwater."

"Okay, Nate Drinkwater, we did you a favor and now it's time for you to reciprocate. I mention Washington, DC because you'll need to go there."

Nate got a sick feeling in the pit of his stomach, the feeling he imagined a hog must get on the way to be strung up and bled.

"The business card?" he asked.

Fiske beamed proudly. "*Verdad*. See, we knew you'd be willing to scratch us back, so we left everything you'd need right there. Here's what you need to do, three things. You ever killed anybody?"

"God, no." The cigarette burned Nate's fingers, and he dropped it into the puddle.

"Well, let's hope you won't need to. It pains me to rely on amateurs, but such is the situation. Anyway, three things. First, find the address. Second, gain entry to the premises and hide in the bathroom. Third, when you hear a group of people—not a single individual, a *group*—enter through the front door, pop out of the bathroom and empty your gun into the ceiling."

"My gun? What gun?" Nate's throat dried up again.

"Oops," Fiske said, smiling brightly. "Getting ahead of myself." He drew his sidearm and laid it on the table in front of Nate. "This gun."

"I hate guns," Nate said.

"I hate people who don't live up to their obligations," Fiske answered, still smiling. "I'm kind of irrational about it."

Nate looked at the gun. The dim greenish light in the room seemed to pool around it and drip from its muzzle. Don't take it, he said to himself. Offer them the money back and they'll let you go.

Except he knew they wouldn't; again he saw himself floating face-down among the barges in the Squatter Regatta. Still he hesitated for a long time before taking the gun.

"I'm not going to shoot anybody," Nate said. His voice shook, and so did his hand as he tucked the gun in his jacket pocket.

"Nate, were you listening? We don't want you to shoot anybody. I told you, that's for professionals. What we want you to do is make some noise, shoot out some ceiling panels. A little chaos injected into the situation. Amateur work, and in this case work requiring a certain anonymity. See, this works out pretty well for you: you're paid in advance and nobody has any reason to connect you with anything. Likewise we remain behind the scenes, which is the way we like it. For now, anyway."

"'Mine hour is not yet come,'" intoned the Bettys by the door. Nate looked a question at Fiske, who shook his head.

"You don't want to know, Nate, believe me. The less you know the better."

"Okay," Nate said. "Guess I'll get along, then. When should I be in Washington?"

He stood, and everyone at the table stood with him. Fiske was shaking his head again.

"Nate, Nate, Nate," Fiske said.

"Tsk tsk," one of the other men said.

Fiske gestured for Nate to sit. Nate did, and so did everyone else.

"We've already made your travel arrangements." Fiske reached into his pocket and took out a flashlight, which he clicked on and pointed across the room. The beam illuminated a steel door like the one Nate and P.K. had come in through.

"In the 1850s there was this thing called the Underground Railroad. Escaped slaves snuck along from point to point, usually up to Canada or up in New England. Out of sight of the Man, right, Nate?" Fiske stood and waved the flashlight at Nate. Nate followed him over to the door.

"Down here," Fiske continued, "we're out of sight of the Man, too. And we're looking for freedom. You like your freedom, Nate?"

Nate nodded.

"I thought so. Well, there are elements in our government that want to take your freedom, and those of us who believe in God and country, old-fashioned ideas like that, have found it necessary to go underground like the old slaves."

Fiske knocked on the door. The hollow sound his knuckles made bespoke a large space on the other side.

"This is our Underground Railroad, Nate. It's bigger than the old one, and it's actually under-ground. The people who built it are all dead, though, so parts of it have fallen into what you might call disrepair. So be careful. Between here and DC there are openings like this one in Newark, Philly, Wilmington, Baltimore, Annapolis…you get the picture. And the number of crazies in those places is pretty freaking high, right, Nate? If you see anyone, your best bet is to put a bullet in them before they do likewise to you. We try to sweep out the nuts every so often, but more always wander in."

"I thought you didn't want me to shoot anyone," Nate protested.

Fiske shrugged. "Self-defense is a special case."

"Oh."

Fiske handed Nate a laminated sheet of paper. "Map," he said. "Side tunnels are generally marked with the addresses of their terminus points. At the bottom of the first stair you'll find a locker. Take whatever you need, and keep an eye out for other lockers along the way. Keys are usually in little magnetic boxes under drainage grates. Also under this stair is wheeled transportation. Washington, DC is 235 miles away, so unless you're in love with fallen arches, I suggest using it.

"Go quickly," Fiske said, opening the door. A damp, cave-smelling wash of air chilled Nate's face. "Today is Friday, right? This thing you're supposed to do has to happen Monday around midnight, and you should get there early. People will be watching the place more in the next few days."

"Where am I going to come up?" Nate asked, staring down into the clammy blackness.

"In a storage room. There are other exits in DC, but I advise against trying any of them. Remember that you owe us a favor, and do not indulge in tourism."

"Do I—should I come back and…what, give a report?"

Fiske waved a hand. "Not necessary. We'll know if you've accomplished what we ask. We'll also know if you don't. A good-faith attempt resulting in failure, of course, is one thing; welshing is another. Remember what I said about welshing."

"How could I forget?" said Nate.

"Don't lose that sense of humor, Nate." Fiske took a step back, bowed and indicated the stairway like a butler. "Good luck."

"Uh-huh," said Nate, and he went down the stairs.

✦✦✦

Nate found the "wheeled transportation," which was a golf cart. Typical military jargonophilia. It clicked on and he took off down the tunnel, trying real hard not to consider what the existence of an underground tunnel from New York to Washington, DC meant in terms of official secrecy, et cetera. He drove long enough that he completely lost track of time, and when he got tired he pulled off and slept. It was cold in the tunnel, but Nate was no stranger to concrete floors. He woke up figuring it was probably Saturday, wished fervently for a cigarette, and drove. God, the tunnel was big. For most of its length it would have accommodated a tank, and side passages branched off every so often to who knew where.

These are the people who have P.K., Nate thought. Ah shit. What did I get him into?

He managed not to think about that for most of the day — well, period of awareness — that he assumed was Saturday. His task was clear. Jump through a door, shoot off the gun, run like hell. I can do that, Nate thought. As long as nobody shoots back.

Well, there was a thought to preoccupy a man. Nate munched it over for what must have been hours, and was so engrossed in his assumption that he was only going to live another two days that when the golf cart's battery died Nate thought he'd just let his foot off the accelerator. He pressed down and nothing happened, though, and all Nate could do was sit there and say, "Fuck. Fuck fuck fuck." He jammed his hands in his pockets and hunched there in the seat, and damned if there wasn't a butt in his left pocket, unbroken and only half-smoked.

Small consolations, he thought, and struck a match.

"Hey there," somebody said.

Nate squealed like a ten-year-old girl and flung himself off the cart. He hit with a crash, lost his smoke, and screamed, "Fuck off! I've got a gun!"

"Me too," came the answer. "The difference is, I know where you are."

Nate froze. "Aw, shit, don't kill me. I didn't want to do it, I don't even know how I ended up here. Don't kill me."

"Relax, I'm not going to kill you. I've never killed anything with an internal skeleton."

"What do you want then?"

"What's your name?"

Whoever it was, he was trying to sound conversational. Nate thought it over. "Nate."

"All right. I'm Bib."

"Bib? Like the thing a baby wears?"

"It's a nickname," Bib said. "My given name's Gabriel. Where you going?"

"Oh, man. Why do you want to know?"

"Tell you the truth, I'm curious. I haven't seen anyone else down here, so I figure you must have some kind of reason. Or were you just taking the golf cart there for a little spin?"

"Well, Bib, I'll tell you the truth. The guys who sent me down here told me that anyone I saw would try to kill me. So I have exactly no reason to tell you anything."

"Look, if I was going to kill you, I'd have done it before you knew I was here. *Capisce?*"

Nate's eyes had adjusted to the loss of the golf cart's headlight, and he saw the glow of a flashlight, dim like it was mostly covered. I could shoot at it, he thought.

"Nate," Bib said, "will you do me a favor?"

"Excuse me?"

"What I'm going to do," Bib continued, "is uncover my flashlight. I won't point it at you. The favor is, I don't want you to shoot me when you see where I am. Okay?"

Jesus Christ, the guy was reading Nate's mind. "Okay," he said.

"Okay. Flashlight coming on." The beam stabbed out toward the ceiling, illuminating a nest of pipes and conduits. Droplets of condensation hung from their joints, occasionally falling out of the light to plop on the floor.

"I appreciate you not shooting me," Bib said.

"Yeah, well. I still could."

"Why? Christ, I could have plinked you when you were coming around that curve, or lighting your smoke, or any time after that. Why do you think I didn't?" Bib stepped slowly out onto the floor of the main tunnel, splashing through a puddle. He was maybe twenty years younger than Nate, and military by the look of him. "Look, if it'll make you feel better," he said, "I'll tell you why I'm down here. As much as I know, anyway. I was supposed to go to New York and talk to the Oracle, whatever that is. Does that make any sense to you?"

126 ◆ Alexander C. Irvine

"The Oracle? Good luck, friend. The Oracle's gone the way of the purple goose."

"Gone? How do you know?"

"I was there last night. There is no Oracle any more, trust me."

"Okay." Bib pointed the flashlight at the floor. "How much do you know about the Oracle?"

"More than you," Nate said. He stood cautiously, saw that Bib didn't have a gun visible, and stuck the gun Fiske had given him into his pocket. "I was going to see the Oracle myself," he said. "But, ah, things kind of went wrong when we got there."

"We?"

"My friend was with me. He sort of got…excused. I'm going to give you the highlights, because I'm kind of grateful that you didn't kill me, but then I'm going on and you're going to have to figure out your own problems."

Bib nodded. "Fair enough."

"I, uh, found some stuff on the street. Some money and other stuff. My friend suggested that we go see the Oracle because the other stuff was…it wasn't exactly ordinary. We went to the Oracle and got jumped by…fuck, you're never going to believe this."

Bib didn't say anything.

"We got jumped by two Bettys, man, or two Bettys and a human, or two humans and a Betty. I'm not sure, but I swear to God that at least one of them was a Betty. They hustled us down under the subway tunnels and there were these guys there. Military guys. They told me I was in a lot of trouble if I didn't do them a favor. So I told them I'd do it."

"Do what?" Bib asked.

"I'm supposed to go to this lawyer's office in DC," Nate said. "There's a—meeting, I guess—that I'm supposed to break up."

"You supposed to kill somebody, Nate?"

"No!" Nate said. "I told them I wouldn't! I mean, they made me take the gun, but I'm only supposed to shoot it at the ceiling or something. Scare everybody off, I don't know." He was near tears now, and he caught himself looking around as if afraid someone was listening in on their conversation. Which for all he knew, they were. Fiske had said he'd know.

"A lawyer's office?" Bib said. "Where?"

"I don't know. One of these tunnels comes up under it. At least they said it does."

"Your lawyer's name wasn't Aschenbrenner, was it?"

Nate wouldn't have thought he had it in him, but he got the gun out and pointed at Bib's head before Bib had even blinked. "How'd you know that?" he demanded, his voice gone all high and trembly.

"Easy, Nate. I'm starting to think we're in the same situation. I've got the Marines looking for me, and God knows who else. A guy named Mike dropped me into this tunnel from Aschenbrenner's office. He told me to go to New York and talk to the Oracle."

Nate lowered the barrel of the gun, just a bit.

"Strange coincidence, huh?" Bib said. "You find stuff in New York and end up headed for DC, I stumble into shit in DC and end up headed for New York. Both of us via a tunnel that nobody knew existed. Nate, does it sound to you like someone hoped we'd meet up and you'd kill me?"

Bib stuck out his hand. "Gabriel Joshua Riley," he said. "How about we go meet this Aschenbrenner and find out what the hell is going on?"

✦✦✦

A side tunnel from the Underground Fairway (Bib couldn't help calling it that after seeing Nate tooling along in his souped-up military golf cart) branched up and ended in a trash compactor set into the back wall of Kaplan, Ng, Aschenbrenner and Ng. The inside of the compactor was grimed with at least an inch of thirty-year-old residue that clung and stunk like automotive grease, and both of them were streaked with black when they climbed out of the compactor's inside door into a storage room piled to the ceiling with bankers' boxes full of dusty files.

"Lawyer's office with a trash compactor," Nate said. "Must have used it to get rid of clients who didn't pay up."

A single ordinary door made of cheap pressboard opened onto an office filled by two desks, some chairs, and floor-to-ceiling bookshelves. Filled with books, even. Four other doors stood closed between the shelves.

Turning back from the doorway, Nate shrugged. "So what do we do now?"

"Dunno," Bib said, shrugging back. "You're the one with the plan."

"Not *my* plan. My only plan is not to end up facedown in a tide pool somewhere."

"Well. So here we are. When's this meeting supposed to happen?"

"Monday night. Midnight, I think."

"Okay," Bib said. "It's Monday morning. We should probably get some sleep."

"Monday morning?" Nate repeated.

Bib nodded. "We walked from, jeez, must've been Delaware. I'm beat, and I haven't been able to tell my wife that I didn't shoot the guy I'm supposed to have shot, and I really hope this isn't some kind of setup, Nate." He sat in the corner of the back room, as far away from the trash compactor as he could get, and fell asleep. Ten minutes later, against his better judgment, Nate was out, too.

Around sunset, Bib woke him up. They cracked the door and took a look around the office space, then peeked through the drawn blinds into the street. The office was in the middle of a block, on a four-lane artery that could have been anywhere in DC out of sight of the Washington Monument. He couldn't see a street sign, and none of the cars or pedestrians gave him anything to pigeonhole the area. Just another city street, baked under the wicked sun and cluttered with trash and anonymous people who didn't know they were anonymous. Nate couldn't see any public terminals, or even telephone. Across the four lanes of traffic was an abandoned movie theater, its cracked marquee proclaiming GOD IS LOVE. Yellowed newspapers covered the insides of the lobby windows, and dozens of posters and handbills plastered the double glass doors. The windows were clear of graffiti, though; the building must have been occupied.

At ten o'clock they crowded into the tiny bathroom set off the storage area. Nate sat on the toilet, leaving Bib to lean against the sink.

"Been meaning to ask you something," Nate said.

"What's that?"

"We've talked. You haven't told me everything, but I know that your wife is gone, you don't know where. People are trying to frame you, maybe kill you. Then you bump into me and get some wild ideas. My question is, Why are you still here?"

"Guess I'm hoping I'll figure out what's going on. Part of it, anyway. Too much weird shit has gone down for it not to be connected somehow. If I can see who's at this meeting, maybe I can get an idea what to do next. How about you?" Bib finished.

"Shit," Nate said. "Three shots into the heating ducts and I'll be gone quicker than a venture capitalist. Hit the tunnels and forget I was ever here. Come up in Rhode Island or someplace."

"Not curious at all, huh?"

"Curiosity's bullshit. Things you need to know tell you you need to know them. Nothing about this fucking mess inspires that feeling." Nate shifted on the toilet seat, resting one foot on the urinal.

About fifteen minutes later, the trash compactor door squeaked open.

✦✦✦

Bound and lying on the floor of an old Dodge van, Nate had nothing to do but listen to the hiss of tires on rainy pavement and hope the clanking gas cans all around him didn't spill too much. A new and entirely original predicament, even for me, he thought. Mugged, homeless, divorced, sure; but never before have I been shot and kidnapped by militant fundamentalists with a paranoid grudge against aliens. Don't think I like it much.

The alien in question, also tied hand and foot, was lying on its side facing him. It looked at him every now and then as if expecting him to say something, but Nate had no idea what that something might be. He'd never spoken to a Betty, and had only seen a handful, when his wanderings through New York took him down around Wall Street or up around the UN. This one looked pretty much like the rest, skinny and pale and disconcertingly similar to humans, except the fishy smell. Bettys reminded Nate of the Eloi from *The Time Machine,* if you skipped the blond-haired part. He didn't think they had any hair at all, except for eyelashes, and the back of the van was too dark to make those out if they were there.

Nate closed his eyes and tried to relax. He hadn't been killed yet, which meant he might not be, and until the situation came to a head the best thing to do probably was rest. Good thing I caught up on sleep back there in the file room, he thought. I'd hate to be a *tired* hostage.

The van hit a bump, jarring the holes in Nate's legs where he'd caught the edge of the load of buckshot that had splattered the crewcut in front of him. He thought he had three pellets in him, none really dangerous (judging by the fact that he was still conscious) but each painful as hell. Blood still trickled along his legs, but the van's suspension was as much to blame for that as anything else. Both legs still moved on command, and he didn't feel like he was bleeding to death. So all things considered, Nate thought he was doing okay.

Another bump and he briefly reconsidered, grunting with pain as the gas cans clanked around him and the Betty. He imagined nefarious microbes creeping into his perforated legs from the van floor.

"I have something I must tell you," the Betty said.

Nate opened his eyes and saw that the alien was staring at him again, its yellow eyes intense and unblinking like a cat's. He wondered what their kidnappers would think about them talking to each other. The back of the van was curtained off by an orange floral-print drapery that hung behind the rear seat, but every so often one of the fundies peeked in on them. The last thing Nate wanted to do was make anyone mad.

The Betty seemed to understand his concern. "I can see the front," it said softly. "If anyone comes, I will stop speaking. All I require of you is to listen."

Sure, I can do that, Nate thought. He nodded.

"I have very little confidence that I will survive this abduction," the Betty said. "If I do not, there is something you must do."

Nate frowned. Listening, that was okay. Doing was something else. The only thing he felt like doing was getting untied and seeing a doctor.

"Gabriel Riley was with you. He is a very important person." The alien stared at Nate.

"Important how?" Nate said finally. Already he didn't like the way he was being led.

Instead of answering, the Betty asked another question. "Why do you think we are here?"

Nate shrugged the shoulder he wasn't lying on.

"All right. Why do you suppose that we can breathe your atmosphere, metabolize some of the plants that grow here?"

Again Nate shrugged. "Anything's possible," he said.

"True, but very few things are likely. I would like to prepare you more thoroughly for what I am about to say, but there is no time. The fact of the situation is this: my people and yours are what you would call related."

Nate didn't know what to make of that. "Related...how? Like family related?"

"In a distant way, yes. A literal translation of our word for you would be 'Cousin.'"

Clearly the alien was serious, but Nate couldn't just accept this at face value. Cousins? All this during a *kidnapping?* "What about evolution and all?" he asked.

"In many places, life is written using a common grammar," the alien replied softly. "We..." It paused, looking up over the seat whose supports dug into Nate's back.

"I think they're talking back here, Henry," one of the fundies said. Nate thought it was the crazy one, the one who thought the Betty was a demon.

As if any of them were sane.

"Let 'em talk," Henry replied. "We've got a long ride, and it won't matter anyway."

Nate didn't like the sound of that.

"I don't know, Henry," the woman said. She was driving, it sounded like; her voice arrived from the wall near Nate's head, while the others sounded like they were talking from his feet.

"Me too," the crazy one—Sam—said. "Why don't y'all shut up back there?" With that he pulled the drape and sat again.

Interesting, Nate thought. They ask Henry the question, but the woman seems to answer. And she was Bib's mother—something was going on there.

The Betty waited several minutes before speaking again, in a voice that Nate could barely hear over the rattle coming from the van's rear axle. He almost wanted to tell it to shut up, but Christ, it was all but revealing the secrets of the universe to him.

Am I getting curious, of all things? Nate wondered. Thought I'd given that up. Then again, how do you know curiosity from what happens when important things announce that you need to know them?

And fuck me if this doesn't seem like something I ought to know.

If he got killed, though…shit. Why didn't they just tell everyone, call a press conference? I'd rather see it on the vid, Nate thought. At Joe Mud's, with P.K. giving me the Gaia-terrorist spin.

"I must tell you from the beginning." The Betty sounded frustrated. Nate expected it to keep talking, but it didn't. Figuring out how to begin? he wondered. Then the van hit a pothole, a real shock-buster, and Nate's vision dimmed as the shotgun pellets danced around in his legs. Blinking tears from his eyes, he saw that the Betty had scooted closer to him, using the noise of the gas cans as cover. Clever alien, he thought, although its sudden proximity made him jumpy. Their knees were touching and the Betty's face was less that a foot from Nate's.

He repressed a sudden urge to kiss it, just to see what kissing an alien would be like. Was it female?

Now that was crystal thinking. Don't lose it, Nate, he warned himself. A little weirdness is okay, considering, but keep your head on.

"Several million years ago, we shared a planet," the Betty whispered, each word slow and distinct. "In a manner of speaking, your species and mine grew up together. Our evolutionary childhood was spent in competition, and for long ages we did nothing more than attempt to survive each other's depredations. But there came a point, when we were at a technological point slightly more advanced than you are today, when our people gained the upper hand. It was within our power to exterminate you."

"But you didn't," Nate said idiotically. He was feeling like Crito, led by the nose through a series of revelations to a conclusion he didn't really want to reach.

"No, although many of us agitated for precisely such action. It became clear to us that as a species, we faced a choice that would define what we were to become. We could eliminate your people, our Cousins, and thereby join the ranks of conqueror races whose ruins litter a million planets. Or we could take a less drastic action, one that would preserve us without destroying you. Clearly our planet could no longer be shared — one of our civilizations alone carried too much ecological weight—but unless we could divert energy from the constant warring between our peoples, we would never emigrate in numbers large enough to save ourselves.

"The choice was made. We collected as many of you as was feasible and assembled transport to take you elsewhere."

Holy Chariots of the Gods, Nate thought. This is like…well, no. It isn't like anything. Every crackpot theory in the history of the world could only be compared to this. But…

"So you just put us on a ship and waved good-bye?" Nate said. "Sounds to me like a more polite extermination, is all." He hadn't thought of it that way, but now that he'd said it, it made sense. Nate started to get mad. As many as was *feasible*, he thought.

"No," the Betty said before he could get too worked up. "We took precautions to ensure, insofar as was possible, that you would survive the trip. We knew, as I have said, that life writes itself according to a limited number of grammars. The ship carrying you had instructions to seek out a compatible planet—one written in the same language, to extend the metaphor, or a close cognate. Your people were placed in what you would call suspended animation, stasis, and sent forth to re-establish themselves on a world where their progress would not be impeded by another sentient race."

"Gee, wasn't that nice," Nate whispered. A thought struck him: The Betty had said millions of years. Nate was no anthropologist, but he wasn't even sure chimpanzees had been around a couple of million years ago. If humans had been such a threat to a civilization that could just pack them up and ship them off like a truant kid to military school, what had happened in all that time? Why hadn't they evolved further? "So if we were so much of a threat that long ago," he asked, "how come we're all primitive now compared to you?"

The Betty sighed. Muscles in its face twitched into what on a human face might have been a frown. "A complex question," it said. "We had no confidence that you would survive the journey in your suspended state, but it was incumbent upon us to make sure you did survive."

"Least you could do," said Nate.

"Our solution was this: using the gene pool of the passengers, we wrote an algorithm that in essence reversed the selection process that had brought you to the advanced evolutionary station you occupied. You might think of it like this: evolution is never linear, and we created in you an attractor that, as long as you voyaged, made the evolutionary impulse in your species work toward what in linear terms would seem like a more primitive state. Your vessel—pardon the negative connotation—devolved the population during the course of the voyage, so that when you arrived you would not immediately overwhelm the local ecology. We have seen evidence of what results when an advanced species colonizes a planet without sentient life. If specific controls are not enacted in advance, ecosystem collapse is extremely probable."

"Rabbits in Australia," Nate murmured. The Betty blinked at him, but went on when he didn't elaborate.

"Perhaps you see our predicament. We had to remove you to save ourselves—and also to ensure that you did not destroy yourselves when you arrived on a new planet—using technology that at the time strained the limits of our civilization. And we also desired that you would arrive without memories of your exile." The Betty made a gesture Nate couldn't interpret. "That last shames me, Cousin. I am not in complete agreement with my ancestors' rationale, nor their decisions. There should have been another way."

"So you turned us back into fucking monkeys and mailed us off to cosmic General Delivery." Nate was glad he was tied up, or else he might have strangled the sanctimonious alien, and then the fundies would have done something crazy. "Well, Christ, at least you feel guilty."

"Guilt, to be blunt, is why we are here." The Betty seemed to recognize Nate's anger, but it did nothing to placate him.

"Here to welcome us back into the family?" Nate hissed. "Well, fuck off. I think we're happier being black sheep."

"That is not our only reason for being here." Still the Betty ignored Nate's fury. Maybe it expected him to react that way, which infuriated him even further. Bad enough to find out that your entire race was some kind of stepchild; being patronized by the older brother was more than he could stand.

"A problem has arisen," the alien continued.

A problem? Nate thought.

"Apparently an error entered into the algorithm, during the second phase. The reversal of the devolution."

Nate opened his mouth, then shut it again as the implications of that statement unfolded in his brain. The idea had been there since the beginning of the conversation, really, but only now did it form itself into words.

"So. We're not...what we were supposed to be," he said numbly. In his mind's eye he saw Eve looking over her shoulder as she reached up into the leafy coolness of the Tree. He pictured what the fundies up front would say if they heard this story.

The Betty was nodding at him, the motion strange because it lay on its side. One side of its bare head was smeared with grime from the van floor. "Gabriel Riley is very important," it said. "He may yet correct the Error."

"He may—"

Someone up front let loose a hoarse scream and the van swerved sharply. Nate's head banged into the seat support and the Betty rolled up against him.

"What!?" the woman snapped. "Sam, I nearly drove off the road!"

"Th—that car, the black one," Sam stuttered. "It's a Betty driving it."

A babble of voices erupted then, and a rain-smelling breeze rippled the drapery and cut the gasoline stink as someone rolled down a window. Nate scooted back, wedging himself tightly as he could under the seat. Some poor sap was going to get shot off the road for being skinny and bald next to a van full of lunatics, and he wouldn't be surprised if they all ended up murdered.

The van accelerated and the orange drapery flew open as Brother Sam lurched into the space behind the last seat. His booted heels barely missed Nate's nose. "Heard 'em talking back here!" he shouted, his eyes darting back and forth between the bound Betty and something over his right shoulder. With one hand he hauled the alien upright and slammed it against the wall over the passenger-side wheel well.

"Who were you talking to?" he shouted into the alien's face. "Who'd you summon, demon?"

The preacher named Henry stepped into view. "Brother Sam, now, you need to calm down," he said, his hands in front of him like he was approaching a tiger without whip or chair. "We're on a mission here, people need to hear what we have to say, and we do *not* need you flying off the handle before we get home! God will provide, Brother Sam, now *calm down!*"

Two shotgun blasts in quick succession rattled a loose bolt by Nate's head. The other Brother must be shooting out the window, he thought.

Sam looked at Henry. He let go of the Betty, which slid down the wall and fell onto its side among the gas cans.

"There's a Betty driving next to us, Henry," he said as if addressing a young child. "Now how did that happen? Is that a *coincidence?*" Sam's voice jumped an octave and veins pulsed in his forehead. "Is that an *accident?* No; demons talk. They talk to each other and we can't hear what they're really saying. And if there's one here, where are the rest? *Where are the rest, Henry?*"

His darting gaze fell on Nate, huddled under the drapery hem at his feet. Nate looked away, but not soon enough.

"Now, Sam—" Henry began, but Sam shouldered him aside. He squatted next to Nate and rested the barrel of his shotgun in Nate's beard.

"You tell me," he said, quiet again. "What did the demon say? Who did it call?"

"Nobody, I don't know—" Nate gagged as Sam jammed the barrel into his throat.

"Tell me," he said again.

I have to live through this, Nate though. What did I do, lift some cash from a dead man about to be ground up for the organ market? I don't deserve to die for that.

"Honestly," he rasped, "I don't know. It wasn't talking to me."

He glanced over at the Betty, lying on its side by the back doors. It was looking back at him, no trace of an expression on it yellow-eyed face. *You understand, don't you?* he thought. *I got your story; I know Bib Riley needs to hear it. The rest I can figure out, but only if I don't die. I'm sorry, but one of us has to. It can't be me.*

Sam stood, and Nate could breathe again. A grim smile deepened the lines around Sam's tombstone eyes; Nate could tell he'd heard exactly what he wanted to hear. "See, Henry?" he said.

Henry leaned against the wall, sweating, his perfect hair in disarray. He opened his mouth, but said nothing.

"This is a war, Henry," Sam said. "It ain't theology no more. Time to cut our losses and run for home."

He stepped over the gas cans to where the Betty lay still looking at Nate. "When you get to Hell, demon, tell 'em Samuel Audette sent you," he said. The alien didn't move as he laid the shotgun on the bridge of its nose and fired.

Oh God, Nate thought. I did that.

From the front of the van, the woman started shouting. "Henry! Sam! Merciful Jesus, what are you doing?"

Henry's gaze was riveted on the gory ruin of the Betty's head. He flinched when Brother Eric fired again up front. The shot that had killed the alien also punched holes through the van's rear doors, and Nate could see blood streaking the bumper and towing ball. Red blood.

Is it true, then? Nate thought. Cousins? I killed my Cousin.

Henry's mouth worked for several seconds before he could speak. "LaWanda," he began shakily, "Sam's—oh my goodness, the gas cans are leaking."

The smell reached Nate's nose as the preacher spoke. He started thrashing against his bonds, ignoring the agony in his legs. Any other way, he thought. Oh God, any other way, but I don't want to burn.

Eric's shotgun boomed again, and the van swerved a bare instant before a shuddering crash drove it further to the right. Gasoline soaked the carpet now, its fumes burning in Nate's eyes as he struggled to sit up.

"Sam!" Eric called. Sam shoved past Henry again. A window broke and both shotguns fired at once.

"What, Henry?" LaWanda's voice cracked. "Speak up, I'm being run off the road here."

Nate wriggled to his feet, using the seat back as support and praying that the van wouldn't suddenly jitterbug again. His legs barely held him up, and he was crying from pain and fear. And sudden, scalpel-sharp guilt.

Henry looked at him, then back at the dead Betty. "I —" he said.

Out, Nate thought. Out now. He worked his way along the wall toward the rear door. I will not burn to death. I don't deserve this.

Henry reached toward him, then pulled his hand back. "LaWanda," he called.

"*What*, Henry?"

Another crash reverberated through the van's frame, followed by the flat bang of a tire blowing out. The van slewed wildly, fishtailing to the right and throwing Nate face-first into the rear doors. Nose bloodied, he came to rest on top of the dead Betty, his left shoulder smeared with what could only be brain. Animal noises gurgled from his throat as he tried again to stand, but just then the fishtailing van hit something and started to roll.

Everything followed with terrible slow-motion clarity. First Nate felt himself collide with the van's ceiling, the impact numbing his legs and setting off a carillon deep in his head. The van's back doors sprang open, and Henry went pinwheeling out, landing just at the edge of the pavement and skipping along like a tin can strung to a honeymooning bumper. Nate saw sparks and a clear arc of spraying gasoline, heard unison screams from the other side of the flapping drape. He crashed back to the floor, heard something crack that might have been a bone; then he was airborne again, his feet banging the van's bumper as he tumbled ass over teakettle into the rainy night, hearing the air-sucking *whoosh* as the van exploded into flame somewhere behind, near, in front of him.

✦ ✦ ✦

He was rescued by another goddamn Betty of all things, and the next thing he knew Nate was in New York telling everything he knew to a Haitian woman named Marie. She seemed worried when the Betty told her LaWanda Riley was still alive, but nobody would exactly level with him, and what with the buckshot in his legs and the fatigue and the general enfucklement of the situation, Nate had purely had it. He wasn't proud of it, but he threw a screaming fit and locked himself in a stateroom on the old casino boat most of the Haitians lived on. They left him alone for a long time, but eventually there was a knock on the door.

It was Bib. Something had changed since the last time Nate had seen him, which come to think of it was only the day before. "I need your help, Nate," he said.

"Forget it," Nate said. "I'm done with this. You people are all crazy."

"Nate, I need you to show me where the Oracle is. Please."

I can't go back there, Nate thought. Fiske is there. There are crazy religious Bettys there. No fucking way.

But Bib just kept looking at him, and Nate started to hate himself.

"Okay," he said. "I'll show you. But them I'm gone, and you all need to leave me alone."

"Deal," Bib said.

♦♦♦

Zena wasn't there when they went down the ladder. The last person Nate saw on the dike was Marie. She leaned down to kiss Bib on the forehead. "You are a good man, Sergeant Bib. What you do today will not be forgotten."

"Take care of Zena," Bib said, and she nodded as she closed the hatch over his head.

They moved quickly through the tunnels, Nate hesitating only as they started climbing a narrow stairway that branched off from the main thoroughfare. "Shit, I hope the door's unlocked," he said. "I'm not sure if I could find another way."

"Everything's worked out so far," Bib said dryly. "Why should we hit a snag now?"

At the top of the stairs, Nate paused. He turned to Bib. "I want you to know that all of us other bastard stepchildren admire the hell out of what you're doing," he said. "Even if I'm the only one who knows it yet. Like Marie said, this won't be forgotten."

"I guess you can never go home again," Bib said. After a pause, he went on. "Mike's probably got this covered, don't you think? I've never killed anyone, and this seems like the wrong time to start."

Nate nodded judiciously. "Mike doesn't strike me as a careless man."

"Yeah."

Nate stuck out his hand, and Bib shook. "This the door?" Bib said.

"It is."

Bib tried the handle. It didn't open.

"Aw, shit," Nate said. "Dammit. How else can we—"

"Like you said, Mike's not a careless man," Bib interrupted. He dug in his jeans pocket and pulled out a key. "He gave me this in DC." A creased photo of Zena had come out of Bib's pocket with the key. Bib put it back without looking at it and turned to the door.

The key turned easily in the lock and the door clicked open. At a card table in the center of the lamplit room sat a small bald man, sunburned and emaciated, his knobby spine sharp against a yellow cyclist's jersey. The heels of his biking shoes tapped on the concrete floor as he jiggled his knees, bent in intense concentration over a hand of solitaire.

"Guess I'll take it from here," Bib said to Nate.

Nate looked past him, into the room. "*Vaya con Dios*, Bib."

"Yeah. You too." Bib walked into the room, shutting the door behind him.

✦✦✦

Nate wasn't nearly halfway back when he heard the explosion as a sustained rumble rolling through the main tunnel. The rumble died away and a breeze came up, a sharp draft flowing north to south. Air leaving, Nate thought. Oh, shit. That means water coming in. He was facing south, so that's the direction he started to run; if he could get to the spur that led under the Regatta, he might just get out.

It's only a mile or so, he thought. Wish I'd talked to the Guinness people ahead of time.

He veered away from a clattering coming from a side tunnel, and just missed being broadsided by a breathlessly excited P.K. Fizer. "Nathan!" P.K. said. "Why am I not surprised? Come on, you're going the wrong way. The tunnel slopes down that way."

P.K. took off north, and a bewildered Nate followed. What was P.K. doing here? It dawned slowly on Nate as Mike's parting words replayed themselves in his mind. Oh my God, he thought. That thing about the truck. He was *serious*.

The wind in the tunnel swirled, died down, changed direction; seconds later, water exploded from the side passage leading up to the Oracle. So long, Bib, Nate thought. Looking over his shoulder, he saw that the tunnel P.K. had come out of was also flooding.

"*Schnell*, Drinkwater," P.K. puffed. "More dike falls down…more water comes in. Faster."

They ran north, hearing a different rumble as they passed near the Amtrak line into Penn Station. Nate wondered if the train tunnels would hold, and as if reading his thoughts — and laughing at them — P.K. cried out, "All aboard, people! Ride of your lives!"

He's crazy, Nate thought. But I guess I've always known that. Water caught them, rose quickly over their knees. In another thirty seconds they were swimming.

"Direct action, yes!" P.K. yelled over the roaring water. "I never thought your friend Mike was serious until he showed up with the truck."

"You're crazy." Nate's thoughts seemed to be reproducing themselves in his mouth. He swam doggedly, with no idea where they were going. His legs, so recently plucked clean of buckshot, were killing him.

"'I am become Death, destroyer of worlds.'"

"What?"

"Quote from the *Bhagavad-Gita*." P.K. spat out water. "What Oppenheimer said at Alamagordo. First A-bomb test. Nowadays anyone can get that feeling."

P.K. caught the edge of a half-filled side opening. "I think this is the one," he shouted. He looked at Nate, a manic grin spreading his goatee into a hairy sunburst. "We'll have to hold our breath, though; it dips a bit before it comes up."

"Comes up where?" Nate remembered that you were supposed to hyperventilate if you had to hold your breath for a long time. He started breathing faster.

"Gas station on 34th and Tenth," P.K. said. "Hope nobody's parked on the manhole. You go first."

Nate sidestroked into the tunnel, still hyperventilating until the roof dipped down and he had to duck under. The passage was narrow enough that he could have touched either wall by extending his elbows, but at least the lights hadn't yet failed and he didn't have to worry about knocking himself unconscious when the tunnel curved up. He followed a gentle downward slope, then maneuvered through a tight question-mark turn. Then the tunnel became a vertical shaft and Nate kicked upward, lungs burning and mind filling with strange memories. He remembered gasoline fumes and not wanting to burn to death, and thought *Stupid, stupid. As if drowning makes you any less dead.*

The water surged under Nate just as he was breaking the surface, and at the same moment the tunnel went dark. Above he saw two tiny spots of light, rushing closer as the water bore him up. He barely had time to cover his head before he crashed into the manhole cover and tumbled out into daylight.

✦✦✦

Nate rolled with the water until he was brought up short against a pump island. He sat up, gasping for air and waiting for P.K. to appear from the upwelling shaft. But the water kept coming, and there was no sign of P.K. Still Nate sat and stared, until an earthquake rumble from the river drew his attention away.

A block down Tenth Avenue, a tidal surge swept through the intersection of 33rd, bearing in front of it a wedge of vehicles, debris and struggling human forms. The wave broke over the jammed traffic, rolling up Tenth to disperse itself through the 34th Street intersection. Nate saw a white bobtail truck with a wedding cake painted on the side and a woman clinging to the top of its cab, skidding down the sidewalk to come up against a steel traffic-signal pole; then he was on the roof of a Jeep, leaping to get a handhold on the concrete awning over the pumps.

The water foamed six feet deep over the gas station parking lot, swamping the shaft Nate had come out of and bringing home to him that P.K. wasn't coming out. It was an irony P.K. would have appreciated, Nate thought, the master plotter swallowed by his most radical solution. He dangled from cramping hands as the Jeep slid away. Up or down, he thought, and grimaced as he pulled himself up and swung a throbbing leg up onto the awning.

He lay there on his belly, watching the torrent shatter the windows of a McDonald's on the opposite corner. Inside, the manager clutched deposit bags with one hand while trying to climb on top of the shake machine. Brown water knocked him down and swept him behind the counter. Framed by the golden arches, the white truck sat like an island, the signal pole jammed into the space behind its cab, brown water rushing around it and eddying around its tires.

"I'll be goddamned," Nate said as he recognized the woman spreadeagled on the roof of the truck. "You're a tough old bitch, aren't you, LaWanda?"

"You know her?"

Nate sat up and turned around to see that several other people had also found their sanctuary on the tar-papered awning. The speaker, a thirtyish blond guy in a Transit Authority uniform, repeated the question. Behind him were two policemen, their riot helmets gone and uniforms soaked and stinking. Both were squinting up at the sudden plague of helicopters.

Over the roar of the flood and the beat of copter rotors, Nate heard LaWanda begin shouting. Some of her words actually reached him: "...on Earth! He died for you!" Christ, he thought, what a banshee.

He wiped a strand of hair from his eyes. "Yeah, I know who she is," he said.

The others drew closer and sat, forming a rough arc in front of Nate. "We saw you come out of the manhole," a pudgy Korean woman said. She held a trembling toddler on her lap, rocking him as she spoke. "Were you down there with Gabriel Riley?"

Nate looked warily at each of them, reminding himself of the promise he'd made. They looked back at him with faces rapt and sincere.

"Yeah," he said. "I was there."

LaWanda Riley's voice shouted on behind him, and a strong breeze buffeted Nate as a FedTV copter hovered close by, a cameraman leaning out the side door to focus on them. Nate looked back to the bedraggled group of survivors, swiped at his tangled hair and took a deep breath. The circle of people drew a little closer.

"Tell us what happened," they said.